He could stay focused on the case, or he could make sure Kara knew she was his top priority, like he should have before. "I've missed *you*," he said finally.

She swung her face away from him.

Three years too late, he thought...but at least he'd finally told her.

She flicked an uncharacteristically shy look in his direction. "I've missed you, too," she said. "Every day."

Ryder's jaw sank open. "What?" He stared hard into her big blue eyes, willing her to say it one more time.

"Every day."

His arms were around her then, pulling her close. The thrill of his heart pounding against hers enveloped him, and when he thought he couldn't take any more, she hugged him back.

Not just a hug. Kara melted into him. "I'm scared, Ryder."

"I know," he whispered, "but you don't be."

MARKED BY
THE MARSHAL

—

JULIE ANNE LINDSEY

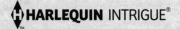

Dedicated to red wine and coffee. I couldn't do it without you.

ISBN-13: 978-1-335-60420-0

Marked by the Marshal

Copyright © 2019 by Julie Anne Lindsey

Recycling programs for this product may not exist in your area.

Printed in U.S.A.

™ www.Harlequin.com

Julie Anne Lindsey is a multigenre author who writes the stories that keep her up at night. She's a self-proclaimed nerd with a penchant for words and proclivity for fun. Julie lives in rural Ohio with her husband and three small children. Today she hopes to make someone smile. One day she plans to change the world. Julie is a member of International Thriller Writers and Sisters in Crime. Learn more about Julie Anne Lindsey at julieannelindsey.com.

Books by Julie Anne Lindsey

Harlequin Intrigue

Garrett Valor

Shadow Point Deputy
Marked by the Marshal

Protectors of Cade County

Federal Agent Under Fire
The Sheriff's Secret

Visit the Author Profile page at Harlequin.com.

CAST OF CHARACTERS

Kara Noble—Ryder Garrett's former fiancée, a new mother and unexpected target of Timothy Sand, the fugitive, arsonist and murderer who came between her and Ryder three years ago.

Ryder Garrett—US Marshal and former fiancé of Kara Noble; he has returned to protect the only woman he's ever loved and her baby from the fugitive who stole everything from him.

Timothy Sand—An arsonist and murderer long on the run, most specifically from Ryder Garrett, currently working to regain Ryder's attention by tormenting his former fiancée and her infant daughter.

Casey Noble—Kara's infant daughter and one current object of the arsonist's attention. A baby in need of a hero.

West Garrett—Cade County sheriff and Ryder's younger brother, willing to do whatever it takes to support his brothers and protect his hometown.

Cole Garrett—Youngest of four Garrett brothers, and a Cade County deputy, Cole is all in to back his brothers and capture the arsonist who is tormenting Kara Noble and her daughter.

Blake Garrett—FBI agent and eldest Garrett brother. Blake's no-nonsense approach to hunting criminals puts him shoulder to shoulder with his younger brothers, determined to protect Kara and her baby at any cost.

Chapter One

Kara tilted her face away from the scalding July sun. It was the hottest, driest summer on record in Shadow Point, Kentucky, and she was eternally grateful for the misty breeze blowing off the fountain at Memorial Park. Her sleeping infant, Casey, on the other hand, seemed utterly unaware that her mother was slowly melting in the afternoon heat. Casey was like that. Naturally content, perpetually at ease. Not at all like the other moms had warned Kara babies could be. Casey had slept through the night by eight weeks and continued to be as lovely and charming as ever at four months.

Kara wiped the back of one sweaty arm across her forehead. A year ago, she'd run three miles before dawn. These days she was lucky to power walk half that before dinner. The heat wasn't helping. She parked the three-wheeled jogging stroller in a berth of shade from an ancient oak and checked her step counter for time and distance. Already 10:00 a.m., and she was a thousand steps shy of her goal. She'd have to make them up indoors. The temperature was rising, and Casey would soon be ready for lunch.

Kara inhaled the sweet scent of blooming flower beds and the busy vendor carts positioned throughout Memorial Park. She eased her backside onto the fountain's wide marble edge and waited for her heart rate to fizzle back to a steady thrum before making the final trek to her car. She gulped the dregs of warm water from her bottle and let her eyes slide shut.

"Beautiful day." A man's voice sprung her lids open. The brim of his dark ball cap was pulled low over his forehead, casting shadows over his wide, deep-set eyes. His dark blue jeans and shirt clung to his bulky frame, likely applied there by a dewy coat of sweat. He clasped his hands behind him and peered into Casey's stroller. "Pretty lady you've got there."

"Thank you." Kara set a protective hand on the stroller's side. She concentrated on Casey's sleeping face instead of keeping eye contact with the man, hoping he'd take the hint. Kara wasn't interested in a conversation or anything else he had to offer. What she needed was to go home and take a shower. Maybe change into something that wasn't soaked in sweat.

"She looks like you," he marveled. "Is her daddy at work? He must be missing her fiercely."

Kara's gut clenched at the thought of Casey's father. A man she'd thought was good and decent, one who'd claimed to love her until a small pink cross appeared on the pregnancy test. Suddenly, he wasn't ready for a life with her. Certainly not prepared for fatherhood. He was sorry, but he just couldn't do it, and how did this happen anyway?

Kara forced the hard rock of emotion down her throat. *This* had happened because she'd allowed herself to let him in, when she knew full well there was only one man in the world meant for her, and it wasn't the man making excuses about commitment.

"No," she answered with more bite than intended.

Casey's father wasn't at work, as far as she knew, and he wasn't missing Casey at all, but that was his loss and Kara's gain. Casey was a gift. Kara knew that now, but for months she'd thought the pregnancy was her punishment for naively letting another man into her life. She figured this was what happened when women were gullible and stupid. The idea, of course, was laughable now. Her pregnancy had been a blessing that changed the shape of her world, and for the first time since the real love of her life had left her, Kara was profoundly at peace.

Except for this guy, contentedly pursuing a conversation, despite the fact that she'd barely looked in his direction. "I'm sorry," she said, looking pointedly at her wrist. "I really should get going. It's time for her bottle, and I want to get her out of this heat." She stood on tired noodle legs and set her hand firmly on the stroller handle. Kara leaned forward, but the carriage didn't budge.

The man had moved his hand to the stroller's opposite side, curling meaty fingers over the edge and effectively holding it in place. "Must you go so soon?" He hitched one side of his mouth into a sinister half smile.

"Yes."

Something dark flashed in his eyes. "May I hold her before you go? Just for a moment?"

"No." The word leapt off Kara's tongue with venomous warning. Adrenaline rushed through her veins, stiffening her posture and renewing her strength. "Please remove your hand from my baby's stroller," she seethed. Her stance widened on instinct and her muscles tensed to fight. It was a new and semi-frightening sensation, but in that moment she was sure she could flatten this man if needed. If he attempted to lay a finger on her daughter, they'd soon find out if she was right.

He stared, unmoving.

"Now," she ground out the word.

Slowly, his fingers pulled away from the stroller. He slid the offending hand into his pocket. The other hung limply at his side. The oily smile she longed to knock off his face had morphed into something like disappointment or distaste. A silver lighter appeared in his hand, pulled swiftly from his pocket. He flicked it to life and watched with the same menacing expression he'd just given her. The flame sputtered, then died with a closing snap of the lid. He tugged the brim of his hat and lifted his gaze back to Kara. "Watch yourself," he warned. "I hear it's going to be an inferno."

With that, he strode away, angling deftly through throngs of parents and caregivers gathered at the little water park nearby. The musical sounds of children's laughter sent a shiver down her spine. The contrast of their happiness to her own fear was unnerving. She watched raptly until he was out of sight, just in case he decided he'd like to hold one of those splashing children the way he'd wanted to hold Casey.

Kara's lungs filled suddenly on a deep intake of air. "Time to go, baby doll."

Casey squirmed at the sound of her mama's voice. A small complaint fell from her tiny rosebud lips. Eyes still pinched shut, she flailed her arms before going limp once more. Someone was due for a feeding.

Kara whirled the stroller away from the fountain, thankful to have left her car parked in the opposite direction from the water park where the man was last seen. If she never saw him again, it would be too soon. In fact, the way her skin was crawling right now, never returning to Memorial Park would be fine by her. Matter of fact, she wouldn't be able to live with herself if that guy harassed anyone else today because she hadn't spoken up. Heaven forbid he lay a hand on any child. The minute they were safely locked inside her car, Kara would call the local sheriff and file a report.

US MARSHAL RYDER GARRETT listened with slow burning fury as his brother West, the Cade County sheriff, relayed a report made by Kara Noble about a strange man at Memorial Park. The fact that someone had upset Ryder's former fiancée was enough to tighten his jaw. The fact that her description of the man in question matched fugitive Timothy Sand had Ryder packing his bags. Even the remote possibility that Sand was anywhere near Kara was enough to send Ryder back to Shadow Point. He hadn't been home in three years, but he was already making plans to obliterate the speed limit on his way.

"She said that?" Ryder asked for the third time, shoving clothes haphazardly into a duffel. "She told you the man said it was going to be an inferno?"

"Yep," West answered. "I remember you saying something like that once when you still lived in town. Your fugitive liked to say it. Any chance he's free again?"

Ryder recognized the leaden weight of failure cooling on his shoulders. "Yes." The word was a knife to his chest. Sand was never put away for what he'd done, and now Kara was in danger because of it.

"I didn't mention it to her," West said. "Didn't want to upset her any more than she already was, but I figured it was worth a phone call to see what you thought."

"To see what I thought?" Ryder snapped. "I think a damn fugitive threatened my—" He stopped short. His what? She was nothing to him anymore, and he'd allowed it to be that way. *Caused it to be*. "Kara."

"All right. So, what happened with Sand? I thought he was arrested."

"He was. Another marshal took over my cases while I relocated a family for witness protection. He caught Sand on a lark. A call to the tip line actually paid off, but the marshal was new and overzealous. He didn't have the right evidence to make his case, and Sand's weasel of a lawyer got the whole thing whittled down to parole and time served." Ryder had been sick when he came back to town and heard they'd had Sand and didn't lock him up. He couldn't eat. Couldn't sleep. Ryder got busy preparing a watertight case against Sand for the murder of Sand's first wife. The crime that started it all. He was darn close to having everything he needed to make sure Sand never saw sunlight. Then Sand's parole had ended, the ankle bracelet had come off and Sand had gone MIA. Until now. "I won't let him get away this time," Ryder promised.

"Well, let's hope that's true. Meanwhile, I can't ignore the possibility there's a murdering arsonist in my county. I put Cole on patrol in Kara's neighborhood and added a deputy to Memorial Park. What are you going to do?"

A low swear slid off Ryder's tongue. He gave his forehead a rough scrub. Kara had unequivocally expelled him from her life. She'd packed his bags and set them on the porch with a note telling him he had to go. Her heart couldn't take watching him waste away any longer in pursuit of one fugitive. It wasn't worth it to her. Was it worth it to him?

Sadly, yes. It had been. Putting Sand behind bars had become symbolic of Ryder's ability to be a marshal, to protect his family, fiancée and anyone else in his charge. He'd bound his self-worth to the apprehension of this man, and he couldn't catch him.

Ryder yanked the zipper on his duffel and slung it over one shoulder. Now he had to go back and protect Kara from a danger he'd inadvertently caused her. West wanted to know what he was going to do? There was only one answer. "I'm coming home, brother."

"Good," West agreed. "For what it's worth, and at the risk of sounding like Mom, it's long past time for the two of you to talk. I hate that Sand is the reason you finally will, but I'm glad anyway. Kara will be, too."

Ryder barked a humorless laugh. Yeah. Kara would be thrilled to see him. He'd stewed in his losses every day, but she'd gone on to find love with someone else, apparently. "Did you say she has a baby?"

West didn't respond. They both knew that was exactly what he'd said.

Did he have to protect the new man in her life as well? His gut fisted at the thought. "How old's the kid?"

"Only a few months. A girl."

Ryder let his eyes drift shut, momentarily frozen in remorse. "She's married, then?"

"Nope. Rumor is that the guy left her when he found out about the pregnancy. That was just over a year ago. Only guy she's dated since you, I believe, assuming the gossip mill's still working fine."

Ryder clenched his teeth. "Best oiled machine in town."

Now there were two men in Shadow Point he wanted to get his hands on. "What kind of jerk does something like that to a woman? To his child?"

"Not one worth having around," West said. "She's better off without him."

Folks had probably said the same thing after she'd kicked Ryder out. They wouldn't have been wrong then, either.

He grabbed his key, badge and sidearm, then headed into the sunset. There'd be plenty of time to fixate on all the ways he'd ruined his life during the three-hour drive back to Shadow Point. Right now, he needed to get moving.

IT WAS AFTER ten when Kara put on her second pot of coffee. It had been twelve hours since her hasty exit from Memorial Park with Casey, and Kara's nerves were still in bundles. Casey, on the other hand, was sound asleep in the nursery. Kara was glad for her, but personally, she couldn't shake the sensation she was being watched.

She'd locked all the doors and shut the windows the moment they'd gotten home. She'd even pulled the curtains in an effort to stop the heebie-jeebies crawling over her skin. Nothing had worked. On any other night, she'd have poured a glass of sweet tea and sat on the porch swing to unwind from her troubles. Tonight, she was a prisoner in her home. A very hot home.

The central air was set to seventy-seven, the lowest she could afford to keep it on her public teacher's salary, and she was dressed accordingly. A worn-out pair of cotton shorts and a pre-pregnancy tank top. The perfect pajamas for nights like these. Though hers were being tested at every seam by the added pounds of stubborn baby weight, she wouldn't complain. Those pounds were hard earned and well worth the prize.

Kara poured a cup of fresh coffee and sank onto a kitchen chair. This wasn't supposed to be her life. If things had turned out the way she'd planned, she wouldn't be shaking the willies right now over some man in the park. She'd be sharing a late-night snack with Ryder Garrett, and laughing as he told her all the ways he could keep that man from ever looking her way again. And he'd mean it. Kara smiled against the rim of her cup. She'd never been afraid of anything when Ryder was in her life.

Let it go, she chastised herself. *You shouldn't want him.* Ryder had chosen a life of compulsion, danger and near madness over her. Based on that alone, she shouldn't love him anymore, but all these years later she still couldn't go twenty-four hours without thinking of him. Ridiculous. Especially since he'd left town and never looked back.

The sound of a car door drew Kara's attention back to the moment, and she was irrationally glad to have something else to think about. Even the possibility of an unwanted guest. Kara padded across the living room carpet for a peek between the curtains. There was no movement on the street or in her driveway. Whoever had arrived or gone in the car had already done so, and the neighborhood had settled back into the hazy calm of a sweltering summer night. She checked the door and window locks again for good measure, moving methodically around the first floor, then up to the second.

It was nothing. Just a neighbor coming or going. No reason to overthink this.

The tug of sleep pulled at her muscles and eyelids as she tested the final window. She rubbed the fine hairs on her forearms, smoothing them where they stood at attention, sent on alert by the goose bumps covering her skin. She'd reported her weird exchange at the park to the local sheriff, a man who had nearly become her brother-in-law once. What more could she do? Thankfully, he hadn't judged her for her paranoia. Instead, he'd promised to look into it and to add a night patrol to her street. She really couldn't ask for more, especially considering nothing had actually happened. Kara had dealt with pushy men all her life, ones who leered at her and said crude things. She imagined all women had, but

it was the first time she'd been confronted so bla-
tantly with her baby present. Maybe that was what
had upset her so much. The idea her baby was there.
That he'd wanted to touch her. *Is her daddy at work?*
Was that his creepy way of asking if Kara was involved with anyone since her ring finger was bare?

Kara moved to Casey's room for another look at
her sweet princess. She needed a nice vision to re-
place the man's face burned into her mind. He'd had
a slightly crazed expression like the one Ryder had
worn at his worst, during the sleepless weeks of obsession over a fugitive named Timothy Sand. Ryder
was barely human in those days, distant and mono-
syllabic. Like an addict or a man coming slowly unhinged. If only. Had either of those things been the
problem, she could've gotten him help, sheltered him
through the storm, but Ryder's problems were of his
choosing, and no one could've put him on another
path, not even her.

Kara stopped the still-turning mobile that dangled
high above Casey's slack face. Baby drool edged from
her droopy bottom lip, perhaps a sign of a first tooth
on its way. One sweet dimpled arm lay across the
stuffed dolly that had once belonged to Kara. Kara
had gotten Rainy Rosie and her little yellow raincoat
in an Easter basket during fourth grade and kept her
in a memory box for years before Casey was born.
Now, Rosie was gnawed on endlessly by her precious daughter. Kara suppressed a chuckle and slid

back into the hallway, tugging the door nearly closed behind her.

The trip back downstairs seemed endless, like a dream hallway that grew longer with every step. Maybe tonight was a good night to sleep in the nursery. She'd fallen asleep in the glider many times before. She could bring a glass of water and a book. Let sleep take her at will.

Kara flipped the light switches and tugged the lamp chains one by one as she shut the house down for the night. Coffeepot off. She poured a glass of water and tucked a worn paperback under one bent arm, then grabbed the baby monitor from the counter. She liked her plan more and more by the second. Locked inside the nursery, she and Casey would be together, and they would be safe. Tomorrow was a new day, and tonight's fears would likely seem as silly as they really were.

She checked the door lock once more and peeked through the front window for the last time. Breath caught in her throat as a tiny movement registered across the street. The glass of water jostled in her trembling hand. Kara shut her eyes and whispered, "It's nothing, there's nothing there, it's okay, you're okay." She reopened her lids and gave the darkened street another cautious look.

Slowly, the shadow of a man peeled away from a broad oak tree and started a path in her direction.

Chapter Two

Kara's pulse pounded in her ears. She pressed a hand to her constricting chest and willed herself to think. The man at the park had been big. He'd had at least fifty pounds on her, and she was out of shape. If he managed to get through the door, no one would see. At least at the park there were a hundred witnesses. Here, alone in her darkened house… Every self-defense move she'd ever learned was gone. Vanished. She could only think of how to escape, keep Casey safe and get away if the man tried to force his way inside.

Heavy footfalls clomped up her porch steps, vibrating through her soul. Where was that extra patrolman West had promised her? *West!* Kara pulled the phone from her pocket and dialed the personal number he'd left with her earlier.

She prayed softly against the phone receiver as the knocking began.

Pick up. Pick up. Pick up. She pressed her back against the warm wooden door for strength and willed West to answer his darn phone.

The knocks behind her came lightly at first, cautiously, and grew steadily more insistent. Her interior lights were already off. Maybe whoever was on her porch would assume no one was home and go away. The nagging possibility she was being paranoid began to creep in. She hadn't gotten a clean look at the man crossing her street. It could be anyone. Maybe she was overreacting. Then again, whoever was out there at this hour was probably up to no good. Man from the park, or someone else. Didn't matter. It was far too late for visiting. Besides, who could it even be? No man had climbed her steps in a year. Figurative or otherwise.

Pick up. Pick up. Pick up. The call connected and Kara gasped. Tears of relief blurred her vision.

"Garrett," West answered, a bubble of laughter in his voice. Country music mingled with sounds of a crowd in the background.

"West?" she whispered, cupping her hands protectively around the phone. Not wanting to be heard by the man outside her door. "There's someone on my porch and I'm freaking out."

The background sounds grew silent. "Kara?" West's voice was sharp now, followed by the distinct snick of a closing door. "What's going on?"

She swallowed a yelp as the knocking grew into pounding against her spine. "Someone's here." The quiver troubling her limbs infiltrated her voice.

Kara swung her attention to the stairwell. She could be upstairs in twenty seconds, and at the back-door with Casey in thirty more. Could the man on her porch break down the door in less time than that? What if he predicted her move and was at the back door when she got there?

"Sit tight," West said with utter Garrett-like confidence. "I'm sending someone to you. Give me five minutes to route him your way."

"Okay." Her darting gaze landed on the hearth. "I might hit him with a fireplace poker."

"Tell you what. Anyone comes through that door without an invitation, and you've got my support in doing whatever you want to him," he huffed. "He's not responding."

"Your deputy?" Kara squeaked. Could the man on her porch have taken out the patrolling deputy?

The knocking stalled, and a new kind of fear clawed through her. At least while he was knocking, she knew where he was. A shadow fell over her front window and the silhouette of a man came into view. "Kara?"

The voice of a ghost permeated her glass. It twisted her core and squeezed her lungs. A strangled noise rose from her parted lips.

"Oh, my goodness." Slowly, she moved away from the door, eyes wide, jaw heavy.

"What?" West barked.

"Kara? Open up," the voice continued, more pleading than stern despite the sharp edge to his words.

She turned the deadbolt and opened the door with bated breath.

"Kara!" West hollered through the forgotten phone in her hand.

"It's you," she breathed.

Ryder Garrett, the ghost of love lost, stood before her in an arch of porch lighting. Hat in hands, he dipped his chin in greeting. "Hello, Kara."

RYDER REACHED FOR her phone and spoke briefly to his brother in acronyms and grunts before returning the phone to Kara.

Kara batted dazed eyes at Ryder before inviting him into their formerly shared home. He accepted with a nod and tried not to wonder what her expression meant, exactly.

She worked her mouth closed, still openly staring at him.

He tried not to return the favor, which wasn't easy. Kara was striking. He hadn't blown her out of proportion in his mind. She really was the kind of woman who could walk down the street and cause a ten-truck pileup. Her pale blue eyes were lined in thick, curled lashes. Her cheeks and lips were naturally pink, though at the moment they were both slightly white from shock. He ached to kiss the line of freckles spilled over her nose. The ones she tried desperately to hide with makeup when they'd gone out for special occasions. He curled his fingers at his side, reminding himself not to touch her. He couldn't do that anymore. It was a privilege he'd lost long ago.

"What are you doing here?" she asked, finally

snapping back to life. She twisted the deadbolt and turned the lock on her doorknob before checking the window.

Did she really think any of that was necessary with him there?

He scanned the vaguely familiar room. Unlike Kara, the home was much different than he remembered. A giant mirror graced the wall above the fireplace where his massive mounted trout had once hung. Their engagement photos and candid snapshots had been replaced with selfies of Kara and an infant. He shook his head. The moment was surreal. It was his home, but it wasn't. She was his girl, but she wasn't. And the baby. Well, she hadn't existed to him until three hours ago.

Kara cleared her throat. "Well?"

Ryder forced a comforting smile. "I heard you had a bad experience at the park today." *Ignore my poor manners for showing up at this hour, unannounced.* He'd dialed her number a dozen times on his drive back to town, but couldn't bring himself to hit Call. What would he have said? What if she'd told him not to come?

Her nose wrinkled. "West told you about the park? Why?"

"He was worried. Thought I might be, too."

"Why?" she repeated. A flash of emotion passed over her stunned expression.

"Maybe you could tell me more about what happened today." He inched toward the kitchen. "We can sit down. Go over the details."

"Okay." She ghosted in front of him. Flipping on lights and starting up the coffee maker. "Coffee?"

"Sure."

Kara kept her back to him as she prepped the mugs. Her head shook infinitesimally, and he was thankful not to know what she was thinking.

He didn't mind the view, either. Being back in this place with her was a lot for him to process. He hadn't anticipated the intensity of it. The sight of their old things. The sound of her grandma's too-loudly-ticking wall clock, and the scents of that sugar-and-spice candle she loved so much. He smiled. In all the years they'd been together, Kara never let their— *her*—personal supply run out. One year for Christmas he'd bought her a case of those candles to be mischievous, but she'd been so pleased that they'd made love right there under the tree. His attention drifted to the exact spot, and heat rose in his chest.

The coffee maker chugged steam into the air, drawing his attention back to the kitchen.

Ryder blew out a long breath and refocused on Kara, but that didn't help clean up his thoughts. And never mind the fact that Kara was wearing a tank top and shorts set that clung distractingly to her new, curvier...everything.

She spun on him suddenly. A frown creased her brow.

He jerked his gaze to her eyes. "What?" Caught ogling. *Real nice.* A true gentleman.

She shook her head again. "West told you that some creep harassed me this morning, and you what? Drove straight here from wherever you live now?"

He nodded slowly. "Cincinnati." That almost summed it up. That and the fact that he believed her harasser to be a murdering psychopath, but there was no reason to say so until he was sure. For the moment, Ryder was enjoying this strange trip into his past. It was nice being there with her. Nostalgic.

Unfortunately, once Kara learned it was probably him who'd put her and her baby in danger, she'd want to coldcock him with that coffeepot.

She made her way to the table, two mugs in hand. The faint scent of cinnamon drifted in the bitter steam. He'd almost forgotten the way she added the spice to her grounds.

"Thanks." He took a seat and waited while she did the same. "Can you tell me everything you told West about the man, plus anything you might've forgotten to mention, but thought of later?"

"Sure, but it's probably nothing. I only called because the park was so busy, and I knew I'd never forgive myself if the guy tried to take one of those other children and I hadn't spoken up."

Ryder's shoulders relaxed by a fraction. "You think he was a child abductor?" Timothy Sand was many awful things, but pedophile wasn't one of them. Maybe he'd been wrong about this.

"I don't know. He leered at me pretty good," she said, looking fairly ill.

"What made you think the man might try to take a child? Did he try to take your baby?"

"No." Kara sipped her coffee. "He asked if he could hold her, but I'd already told him we needed to leave. It was really weird. Then, he put his hand on the stroller for a minute when I tried to go, but he relented, and he never threatened us. I just had this feeling." She fisted a hand against her gut. "You know?"

He did. Instinct had told her that man was dangerous, so he probably was. "Start from the beginning."

She set her cup down and stared into it. Slowly, her lids slid shut, and she began to recount the exchange in unbelievable detail. A hat had hidden the man's hair and shaded his eyes, but she was certain they were both brown. He was clean-shaven, and she'd noticed acne scars along his cheeks. There was a tattoo on his left wrist. A single black heart.

"Observant." Pride bloomed in Ryder's chest. They used to test one another about the little details around them. She'd enjoyed the game more than he did because despite his flashy badge, she'd usually won. She claimed being a kindergarten teacher made paying attention to the details especially necessary.

Kara opened her eyes and lanced him with her careful stare. "I'm glad you're here, Ryder. You look good, and I'm glad to see you this way again."

He didn't have to ask what she meant by "this way

again." He knew. *Healthy. Rested. Fed.* The last time she'd seen him, he was a shell of himself, obsessed with the one that had literally gotten away. He didn't eat or sleep in those days, and he was pretty light on the showers and speech. He'd spent every hour fixated on Timothy Sand and his capture. Ryder raised his mug and blew across the fog of steam. "Thanks. I took your advice. Got some help."

Agency-mandated help, but still.

He'd lost control and laid a fist into the new kid who'd brought Sand in but failed to keep him in jail because of the flimsy case he'd prepared. Ryder had been temporarily relieved of his badge and sidearm after that. It was the lowest point of his career. The lowest point of his life had been two months earlier, when Kara told him to pull it together or leave.

The suspension eventually opened his eyes to how far he'd fallen down the rabbit hole. Mandatory sessions with an in-house therapist had helped him get his life back together. By that time, it was too late to come home to Kara. His mind was clear, and he finally understood how much he'd hurt her. She deserved better than that.

"You ever catch that guy?" she asked. "What was his name—Timothy Rand?"

"Sand," Ryder corrected. "Timothy Sand. No. I never did."

She twisted her mouth into a sad smile. As if to say, *It was all for nothing, then*. A broken engagement. Two broken hearts.

Ryder cleared his thickening throat. "How about you? You're stunning as ever. Motherhood's been good to you, I see."

"Thanks." She dropped her attention away from him, and a blush darkened her cheeks. When she dragged her gaze back to his, she smiled. "She might be the best thing that's ever happened to me. I never expected I'd be a single mother, but she's worth it, and I know we'll be okay."

Kara was strong. He'd never let the kindergarten-teacher front fool him. She could command armies if needed. "And the father?" Ryder forced the last word through his teeth. No one who abandoned his woman and unborn child deserved a title like that. But what else could he call him. Whoever he was.

"Gone." She pulled in and released a long, steady breath. There was no remorse in her face, no anger. She was a better person than Ryder. The man hadn't done a thing to him, and he wanted to punch his face.

"Does he check in from time to time or…"

"No," she interrupted. "Like I said. He's gone."

"I'm sorry to hear that." And he was. Because if the guy was here, he could hit him.

"Thanks."

West had it right on this one. Kara was better off without a man who'd leave her like that. Ryder settled back in his chair, stretching booted feet beneath the table. He and Kara were about as caught up as they could get without unloading the massive elephant from his pocket. He set his phone on the table and flipped quickly through the photos he'd downloaded after speaking with West tonight. "I've got a photo of a fugitive I'd like you to look at."

Kara stiffened. He could almost see the lightbulb flicking on as fear bleached her freckled cheeks. "You think the man who talked to me is a federal fugitive?"

"It might be nothing." He forced a lazy smile. "Maybe your guy was a run-of-the-mill weirdo."

She lifted crossed fingers in a show of sarcasm. "Let's find out."

Kara raised her chin in agreement. "Okay." She opened her hand to him. "Let's see it, then."

Ryder turned the little screen to face her. "Do you recognize him?" The photo of Sand was nearly two years old, and the most recent surveillance the US Marshals had. He wore a bushy beard and full head of hair in the picture, nothing like the description she'd just given him.

"That's him."

Ryder's gaze jumped to hers. "You sure?" His heart pumped strong and hard against his ribs. "This is the man who bothered you today? You said he was clean-shaven and wore a hat. How can you tell with the big beard and wild hair?" He even had sunglasses in the gas station photo.

Kara set one pale pink fingernail on the grainy image. "There."

Ryder turned the screen to him for a closer look. The photo showed Timothy crossing the parking lot, legs extended in midstep, tucking cash into his wallet. One wrist in full view of the camera, with a small black spot marking him for the marshal.

She leveled Ryder with a no-nonsense look. "I'm willing to bet you'll see that's a heart if you blow up the image. Now, it's your turn."

Ryder stared at the photo. Sand didn't have a tattoo. Did he? If so, he'd gotten it since the last time Ryder had laid eyes on him, and he hadn't noticed it in this photo until now. Because he hadn't expected it, the spot had seemed to him like nothing more than a digital blemish, but Kara's description and the placement of that mark were too coincidental.

Ice rolled through Ryder's veins. Timothy Sand was in Shadow Point, and he knew who Kara was.

"You want to tell me exactly who that man is?" she asked, arms folded on the table. "And why a federal fugitive whom you're hunting sought me out in a park bursting with people?"

Ryder pulled in a deep steadying breath. "I can only guess at how to answer that last question."

"And the first?"

Ryder dropped the phone between them. "This man is Timothy Sand."

Chapter Three

Kara's eyes bulged. Her heart lodged in her throat. "No," she said, unwilling to allow the vile statement to be true. "He *can't* be." She pressed her pointed finger against the tabletop. "No."

Ryder rubbed his mouth and lightly stubbled cheeks, a look of apologetic desperation in his eyes. "Kara," he began.

She shook her head, cutting off whatever he'd planned to say. "Unless the next words out of your mouth are going to be 'Just kidding,' then keep 'em to yourself." Her traitorous lip quivered and tears stung her tired eyes. There had been far too much drama today. Too many men. They were ruining the peaceful, predictable, nearly perfect life she adored. She and Casey were supposed to be safe in Shadow Point. Supported by the community. Surrounded by a tight network of moms she'd met in Lamaze and Stroller Fit classes. Things were going really well, and now… her gaze fell on Ryder's handsome, bunched up face. "You can't come strutting back into my life after years of doing who-knows-what and mess it all up. I won't allow it."

His jaw dropped. The startling blue of his eyes seemed to darken in disbelief. "What do you mean? *Who-knows-what?* What do you think I've been doing?"

She crossed her arms in a show of defiance, but fear was already sliding over her, jarring her composure. "I can't do this." She dropped her tone and petulant posture. "Not anymore. I put you and your Sand obsession out on the curb. You can't just pop back up. My heart can't take it." She rubbed her chest. She shouldn't have to worry about protecting her infant from a fugitive, and she shouldn't have to endure the pain of watching Ryder walk away again when his business in Shadow Point was done.

Her arms found their way back around her middle, uselessly trying to hold herself together while a tornado of emotions spun in her scrambled head. How stupid of her to feel heartbroken all over again. The sight of Ryder Garrett shouldn't do this to her. It wasn't right. Wasn't fair. She bit into her lip and forced herself to think rationally. Ryder wasn't back for her. He was back for Sand. He'd landed on her doorstep dragging the same baggage he'd left with. Only this time everything was worse. The fugitive was in town. And she had a baby to think about.

She narrowed her eyes at Ryder, measuring what to say next. She should never have let his clear expression and sensible words fool her. He wasn't reformed. Ryder was still a junkie. He might not be hooked on anything illegal, but his drug of choice was every bit as lethal.

RYDER WATCHED HELPLESSLY as Kara's wide eyes brimmed with tears. Never one for a big show of emotion, she shoved away from the table and turned her back on him. He followed her to the living room on instinct. "Kara." This was 100 percent his fault. He'd somehow allowed the monster he'd chased for so long to wind up on her doorstep. Whether or not Sand had made a personal appearance at her home, he'd found her at the park, and that meant he knew her routine. He'd likely been watching since the first day he was set free. "I'm sorry."

She stopped midstep and turned on her toes to face him. A solitary tear rolled over her cheek, but she made no move to catch it. Instead, her stubborn chin inched higher. "Why?" she snapped.

"Why what?" Ryder froze, mentally flailing. "Why is Sand here? Bothering you? I don't know, but I promise you, I *will* stop him this time."

She puffed out her cheeks, sending air into her bangs and setting them to flutter. "*Why* are you sorry?" She dragged the question into long, pointed words.

Ryder rocked back on his heels. A boulder of regret settled in the hollow of his chest, flattening his lungs and strangling his breath. He slid his fingers into the front pockets of his jeans. When he'd followed her to the living room, he'd intended to hold her, to cradle and comfort her, but the look on her face said he'd likely lose a hand for trying, and he'd better start talking or he was going back to the curb, fugitive or not. "I'm sorry for everything." He cringed at the lame answer. He knew it wasn't what she wanted, but it was true anyway.

"Keep talking."

"All right." Might as well start with the most obvious and pertinent reason. "I'm sorry my position as a US marshal has upset your life and possibly endangered you and your baby."

Her eyebrows rose in unison. A perfect expression of *You think?*

She turned to pace the room, aimlessly righting toppled piles of plastic toys and stacks of small pink blankets. "Anything else?" she prompted, suddenly abusing a frilly pillow.

"Yeah, but I don't think this is the right time to talk about that." In other words, he didn't know where to begin, and he'd rather not. He'd imagined contacting her a thousand times, even rehearsed in the shower what he would say to her, and, embarrassingly, once to his therapist at work. It hadn't been his intent to talk about Kara, but there was only so long he could discuss punching his coworker in the face.

Kara snapped upright, dropping the little pillow onto the couch. "Now's not good for you, huh?" She nodded slowly, baiting him. "Well, a better time, then." She glided around the coffee table straightening magazines. "I wonder when that will be?" She tapped her chin thoughtfully. "Maybe two or three years from now when you turn up without notice again? Will that work for you?" She smiled, tight and bright. "I can't imagine what the reason will be next time. Maybe a crime boss on the run will be posing as my daughter's preschool teacher."

Ryder's lips twitched. He'd always gotten a kick out of Kara's fury. Not that she was usually wrong in her anger. She was patient and forgiving to a fault, but she was also stretching for five foot four, and her long wavy blond hair and big cartoon princess eyes made it all the worse. Angry Kara was a fluffy bunny baring her teeth, and the sight of her tiny face turning six shades of pissed usually ended their fights. He'd laugh, apologize and drag her into his arms, because what kind of jerk upsets a bunny?

Kara's forced smile fell. She pressed her palms against the narrow curve of her waist, emphasizing her full breasts and testing the integrity of her tank top. "Something funny?"

He pulled his eyes back above her collar where they belonged. "What?"

"Why is the fugitive you were chasing three years ago bothering *me* now? To hurt you? That seems silly. If he thinks we're still a couple, he should brush up on his stalking skills."

"I imagine that's what he's doing now. I think you're right. He's looking to hurt me, and now he's free to do it."

Kara's knees buckled. She planted onto their old couch with a sharp exhale and covered her lips with narrow fingers. "He asked me about the daddy."

"What did you say?" A bubble of hope rose in Ryder's chest. "Did you tell him the father's name? Make sure he knew she wasn't mine?" Maybe Kara and her baby were safer than he'd thought. Sand was sure to leave Kara alone if he knew she wasn't in Ryder's life anymore. He'd have to move on. Find another angle.

Kara stretched her eyes wide. "I didn't tell him anything. He asked if her daddy was at work, then he said he must be missing her. I just said no. I don't engage with people like that, and I never give out personal details. I made it crystal clear that my level of interest in talking with him was zero, and I left."

Ryder swore, then pinched his lips tight. He ran a heavy hand through his hair and curled his fingers knuckle-deep into the strands. Kara had done the right thing for any other situation, but she'd likely only kindled Sand's interest today. They were engaged when Ryder started to pursue him. Sand had no reason to think they weren't married now and raising a family.

"S-so," Kara stuttered. "Sand is definitely coming after me now because he thinks we got married and had a baby."

Ryder took a seat at her side and swooped an arm around her shoulders like he had hundreds of times before. "Come here."

She leaned into him, covering her face with one hand and rolling against his side. He inhaled the soft, familiar scent of her, soaked in her warmth and longed to be her hero once again. The man she'd fallen in love with when he saved her goofy kite from a tree. Her class had finger painted terrible kites to look like butterflies and rainbows. An errant wind had blown Kara's into a tree. If it hadn't been for that damn kite and Ryder's affinity for tree climbing, they might never have met. But they did, and they were happy.

He missed being there for her. Opening jars and carrying things her short little arms couldn't manage. He missed driving her places in his truck so she could perform a one-woman karaoke concert in the passenger seat. More than that, he desperately missed *her*.

Kara pulled her legs onto the couch, hugging her knees to her chest and pulling away from him. She folded herself into a little bundle, and Ryder longed to toss her in his truck and rush her to safety.

But she had a baby now. And a life here without him. He couldn't carry her away.

He had to stay and protect her. He needed to fix the mess he'd inadvertently caused. "Hey." He set a careful hand on her back and rubbed the pad of his thumb against her shoulder blade. "I know you don't have any reason to believe this, but I'm not the same as I was before. My head's clear. My priorities are straight. I've never been better at what I do, or knowing who I am. I can catch Sand this time, and when I do, I've got enough evidence to form a pretty strong case against him for his first murder."

She rolled her head against her knee until her face came into view. Her lashes were wet with tears. "Yeah?"

"Yeah." He curled a swath of her hair around his finger and tucked it behind her ear, keeping his eyes fixed on hers, begging her to see the truth. He could and would protect her at any cost.

Kara nodded. "Okay."

"Good," he whispered, emotion choking the word. He opened his arms and she fell right in, collapsing against his chest and curling into the curve of his side. Kara believed him. Despite everything they'd been through, and despite seeing him at his worst, she trusted him to protect her and her baby. That meant something. His heart swelled with joy and hope for a different future. "I won't let Timothy Sand hurt you," he said, stroking her soft vanilla-scented hair. "That's a promise."

SQUEALING TIRES BURNED a hole in the comfortable silence and Kara's limbs went rigid.

She yelped as Ryder swiftly shoved her aside. He leapt away from the couch before the raucous sound had ended. "What is it?" She jumped onto her feet a split second behind him, but Ryder was faster, already out her front door and jogging down the street.

A pair of glowing red taillights were barely visible in the distance.

Kara shut the door and locked it. She grabbed the baby monitor from the counter and found a place at the front window where she could watch whatever happened next. Should she call West? Or make a run for the nursery to collect her baby?

Outside, Ryder strode confidently through the night, gun in one hand, cell phone in the other.

Maybe he would call West.

He stopped at a large SUV parked catty-corner from her home and holstered his weapon. He turned in a small circle before lifting something from the vehicle's windshield.

Kara strained to see what it was.

Ryder made another call and headed back in her direction, moving slowly at first, then breaking into a jog.

As he passed beneath the motion light over her driveway, the mysterious object came terrifyingly into view.

Someone had left Ryder a badly charred matchbook.

Chapter Four

Kara unlocked the door and stepped away as Ryder turned the knob. He walked back inside unbidden, a sadly appropriate metaphor for their relationship. All he had to do was show up, and she let him in. He dropped a black duffel bag onto her floor, apparently planning to stay awhile. She shook her head, silently scolding herself for the naive flutter of excitement. Ryder Garrett might offer protection from whatever he'd gotten her into, but he was dangerous for her heart. Just seeing his face had quickened her pulse, and the way she'd felt while briefly in his arms tonight had brought an unwelcome rush of nostalgia.

Nice as it was to think things could be different, she couldn't allow Ryder's presence to shift her world in unfair ways. And she couldn't afford to let her foolish heart distract her from the real reason Ryder had shown up at all.

"Well?" she asked, wrapping goose-pimpled arms around her middle and eyeballing the charred matchbook in his hand.

He rubbed the sleeve of his black jacket across his forehead. "Can I borrow a baggie?"

Kara glared at him before marching into the kitchen.

Ryder followed, tapping away at his phone screen with the thumb of one hand, while carrying the ruined matchbook, reverently, in the other. The crazed look on his face tilted her stomach.

"Is that from him?" she asked, as if the answer wasn't obvious.

"I believe so, yes."

She swung the pantry door open and tried not to vomit. Kara had been afraid of many things in her life, but never *for* her life. Certainly not for the life of her daughter. Her gut clenched more tightly at the thought.

"Here." She thrust an empty sandwich baggie in his direction, half terrified, wholly pissed. "Will this work?"

"It's fine."

"Are you sure?" she snapped. "Because as far as I know, it's only meant to hold the innocuous parts of my lunch. Not the charred remains of a serial arsonist's blatant threat."

Ryder dropped the matchbook into the baggie and zipped it shut. "Don't sell him short. He's also a murderer."

Kara's jaw dropped.

Ryder grimaced. "Sorry. I just can't believe this is happening."

That makes two of us.

When Kara had woken this morning, her biggest concern was fitting back into her pre-pregnancy wardrobe before school started next month. She'd feared having to buy more clothes on an already tight budget and leaving her baby for the first time since seeing her sweet face in the delivery room.

Now, thanks to some evil twist of fate, she and Casey were on a lunatic's radar when the man he truly wanted was in her kitchen unpacking what looked like an overnight bag.

Cruel fate had to keep twisting that knife a little deeper. Taking Ryder from her, then returning him only because his criminal obsession had visited. Now, to require that he stay with her, in the home they'd once shared. Kara rubbed the heated skin above her heart, unable to soothe the deep ache.

"Ryder." She placed a hand on his shoulder as he unearthed a small fingerprint kit and gloves from a compartment beside a change of clothes.

Her hand slid off as he set up a makeshift workstation on her countertop, unhearing, then adjusted a lamp to shine on the area. The efficiency of his quick movements was all too familiar. Kara recognized the stiff posture and focused expression as he entered what she'd grudgingly called "marshal mode." A chill slithered down her spine, sending a mass of ugly memories to the surface. The gut-churning recollections of watching helplessly while her fiancé became consumed rolled her stomach.

"Ryder," she repeated, using her teacher voice this time.

His face jerked in her direction, and a look of shock raised his furrowed brows. Had he already forgotten she was there?

"Yeah?" he asked, seeming to return to himself. His ruddy cheeks and clear eyes were an improvement over the last time she'd interrupted him like this.

A bud of hope grew in her heart. Maybe Ryder was telling the truth. Maybe he was better now. Much as she wanted to believe it, she had more than herself to worry about. She had to think of Casey's best interest and not her own desperate heart.

Kara moved forward, pressing into his personal space and leveling him with her business stare. "Stop."

He dropped his hands to his sides and turned to face her fully, leaving the project to wait. For a moment, he looked frightened, as if whatever she said next could have the power to break him.

Somewhere deep down, Kara thought that might be true. After all, Ryder had loved her once, just not enough, and never more than his fixation on a man who didn't know he'd existed.

Kara pushed hurt feelings and pride aside. Everything that had happened between them was in the past. Right now she needed to know why Timothy Sand had approached her and how to keep Casey safe.

Right now, Kara needed a partner.

She lifted her brows at him. Ryder wouldn't want to answer her next demand, but he had to. The moment his job had put her daughter in danger, Kara earned the right to know exactly what she was dealing with.

She tipped her chin upward and squared her shoulders. "I need to know everything there is to know about Timothy Sand."

RYDER TRIED HIS best not to argue. He needed to at least attempt to pull prints from the matchbook, but she was right. He also needed to help Kara understand the things he'd never told her before. When they'd been in love, he'd worked hard to shield her from his work. It didn't involve her, and Ryder had wanted to protect her. Kara was sweet-natured and kind. The sort of woman everyone loved at first sight. It didn't make sense to ruin that with stories of fugitive apprehensions or prisoner transports. She didn't need to know all the awful reasons people lived in witness protection, or why serving federal arrest warrants wasn't as simple as what was portrayed on TV.

He'd intentionally kept the details of Timothy Sand's crimes out of their pillow talk and dinnertime conversations because Kara was too good to hear that mess. She was good and true. Timothy Sand was something evil.

Ryder poured two fresh cups of coffee and sent another round of messages to his team in Cincinnati on his way to the table where Kara waited. He'd protected her before. The gruesome details had had nothing to do with her. But things had changed.

He settled into the chair across from her at the small dinette, hating everything he had to say next almost as much as the man it was about. Timothy Sand had given him no choice but to reveal the sequence of events that had nearly driven Ryder insane.

"Just say it," Kara blurted. "I can take it. I just need to know. No more secrets or you're not staying."

Ryder patted the table with one heavy palm. He was staying whether she liked it or not. It might be in a sleeping bag on the porch, but he wasn't leaving. Not until he could take her with him, which would hopefully be in the morning.

"Timothy Sand is an arsonist," he said. Kara knew that much, of course. She tipped her head sarcastically, as if to say, "No kidding." "He set fire to the home of his in-laws after his wife ran there for refuge."

She sat back then, obviously feeling the weight of his words. Her lips pressed into a thin white line. Domestic violence was a personal villain of Kara's. An ex-boyfriend in high school had hit her after she didn't "act right" in his opinion. She didn't talk about the details often, but she'd made it her mission that day to shed light on people like him and expose abusive men for what they were: criminals.

Ryder had been very careful to make sure she knew he wasn't like that guy. He'd have gladly stepped in front of a train to protect her. Still would. And anyone who wouldn't didn't deserve her time.

"And?" she prompted, coming back to life after the initial jolt.

"He'd been charged with multiple counts of domestic violence over the years. Eventually, his wife had enough and left him. You know the statistics on that." Leaving an abuser often escalated the abuse. Timothy was no better than the average aggressive asshole. No. He was much worse.

Ryder wrapped his hands around the nearly forgotten mug of coffee. "He followed her to her family's home where she went to hide. Then he killed her, her parents and her younger siblings with a hunting knife."

Kara covered her mouth with one small palm.

Ryder's face heated with residual anger, and he felt the disgust rise inside him. He hadn't captured Sand when he had the chance and now that monster was after Kara.

The look on Kara's face was so heartbreaking Ryder considered ending the story there. He hated being the cause of that expression. The one that said, *How can you deal with this every day? It's unthinkable. Vile. Horrific. Disgusting. What kind of person chooses this work? Chooses to expose themselves to these things without end?*

All legitimate questions, but what most people didn't understand was that there were days when everything was golden and the bad guy paid for his crimes because of people like Ryder. Days when a family was released from their personal hell because a fugitive was captured. A killer put in jail. Those days made all the bad ones worthwhile.

"Timothy Sand burned the house down around their bodies, making it harder to identify them and the causes of their deaths, but there will always be a few things that can't stay hidden."

"The sun, the moon and the truth," she said.

Ryder nearly smiled. It was nice to know she remembered his family's favorite saying. Four brothers and a father, all lawmen. All who believed in justice and vowed to serve as best they could to make it happen.

"Sand was caught, eventually. He had no remorse. Probably blamed his wife for running and the family for giving her shelter. He's still wanted for the original charges plus multiple counts of murder and unlawful flight to avoid prosecution when his path crossed mine."

Kara listened intently. "'Multiple counts of murder to avoid prosecution,'" she repeated. "Does that mean he killed again, while you were chasing him?"

Ryder nodded.

"And that was when you got hooked. Trying to stop him."

"Yes." *Hooked.* She'd always used that word as if Ryder had been on drugs. Though, in hindsight, it wasn't the worst analogy. He'd been just as addicted, just as sick.

"That was the beginning," he admitted. "After a while, I made some progress tracking him, and things got worse. I followed him to a small town in Ohio."

Kara crossed her legs and leaned closer. "You were gone two weeks. I remember."

"I had him." *Almost.* Ryder swallowed hard, forcing his shameful gaze back to Kara's sincere one. He'd driven through the night to get there, then followed the leads right to Timothy Sand. Within forty-eight hours, he knew everything he needed to bring him in. "I walked the town. Talked to the locals and uncovered his one mistake. He'd used his real name with a convenience store clerk, Jennifer Sayers." Ryder's lids fell shut. When he reopened them, he focused on the details of his old kitchen instead of the beauty before him. "Jennifer was young, happy and pretty enough that he'd forgotten himself, forgotten the alias. That slip was all I'd needed to get my hands on him."

But he hadn't.

Instead, Ryder had lurked in the shadows, building his case and waiting for the right time to make his arrest. "Three days after I'd started following him there, about a week after I'd received the notice that someone fitting his description was in that town, I went to the docks where he worked under an alias and waited for him to return from lunch. There were plenty of witnesses on hand, and he had nowhere to run without going for a swim. He took a bus to work, so there was no getaway car. Just a marshal and a fugitive. It should have been a textbook capture, but Timothy never showed. Instead, he went into town during his lunch and burned down the home of Jennifer Sayers."

Kara gasped.

Ryder pressed on. "Somehow, he'd known I was there. Knew she'd told me about him. And he went to punish her." Ryder pressed angry fingers to his temples. "She had an infant and three other children with her in the home."

Shock twisted Kara's sad expression into something caught between pity and horror.

Ryder couldn't blame her. He'd felt those things and more when he'd gotten the news, until eventually he'd felt nothing. In fact, the aftermath of that fateful day had nearly killed him. Thankfully, punching his colleague six months later had resulted in him getting some help. All those weeks of Marshals-mandated counseling should have been a joke, but it became his lifeline.

"That was when I began to unravel," he admitted. He dragged his gaze back to hers, hating what his hesitation had done to the lives of Jenifer Sayers and her family. To Kara's. To his. "For me, that was the beginning of the end."

Kara set her fingers over his hand on the table and warmth spread through him. "Hey."

Ryder raised reluctant eyes to hers. "I'm so sorry."

Kara nodded once. "I wish I had known."

"I couldn't say it out loud," he whispered. "When I came home to my happy life. My fiancée. Planning our wedding." He swallowed long and slow. "Everything Jennifer had lost because I didn't act faster…"

Kara's fingers curled under Ryder's palm. "If he's in Shadow Point, I know you'll find him. You can get him this time."

Ryder forced a painful lump of emotion deep into his chest. "I will."

"Okay," she said. "Should I guess from the duffel bag that you'll be staying here while you're in town?"

He glanced at the couch. "If it's all right with you, I'd rather not leave you alone. Tomorrow I'll find a better place for you and your baby until Sand is captured."

Her panicked gaze jumped to the baggie with the charred matchbook. "You don't think I'm safe here? You think that guy might burn my house down?" Kara was on her feet then, hands waving helplessly in front of her.

Ryder met her there in an instant, and he wrapped her in his arms. The fear on her face ripped at his already shredded heart, and he did the only thing he could in that moment. *Be there for her.* Shockingly, she let him. "I'll protect you, Kara," he vowed. "You and your baby. We'll move you someplace safe tomorrow, but right now there's work to do."

Kara wriggled free, wiping her eyes and staring anywhere except at Ryder. "Right. I'll go pack my things and a bag for Casey so we're ready."

Ryder nodded, already back to the island and setting up to check the matchbook for fingerprints. "I'll call and make arrangements for the move."

The baggie fell from his fingertips then, caught by the counter beneath his hands. He turned to gape at Kara as she hustled toward the steps to the second floor. "What is your daughter's name?" he asked, projecting his voice so Kara was sure to hear.

Her cheeks went crimson. Her feet slowed on the carpeted stairs. "Casey," she repeated, a pained look in her eye, before hurrying out of sight.

Ryder Casey Garrett worked to reinflate his lungs.

He'd been gone far too long to be the baby's father, but maybe Kara hadn't written him off as completely as he'd imagined. Maybe there was still hope there.

Chapter Five

Ryder watched, dumbfounded, as Kara disappeared up the steps.

The buzzing of a new message on his phone pulled him back to the task at hand. West was waiting for photos of prints taken from the matchbook. He'd promised Ryder access to the county's lab and anything else he needed while he was in town pursuing Sand.

Ryder didn't have to work hard to get prints. It was as if someone had deliberately pinched the book between a thumb and forefinger, intentionally leaving clear and blatant marks. He didn't need the prints to know Sand was in town. Kara had confirmed that with the photo, but physical proof would allow Ryder to stay and hunt him. His caseload was too full to take a side trip on a hunch. These prints were a permission slip to stay. Without them, he'd be unemployed because he'd sooner quit the marshal service than leave Kara and Casey alone in a town with a killer.

The knots in his already twisted stomach pulled tighter.

Sand knew who Kara was *and* where she lived.

Ryder snapped the digital photos, then sent them to his brother, jaw clenched and teeth locked. The sonofagun had crossed a line, and he wasn't getting away with it.

"Everything okay?" Kara reappeared in a baggy T-shirt and pajama shorts. She lined a row of neatly packed bags beside the door. Some were familiar pieces she'd once taken on their trips together. Others were new, smaller and covered in pink polka dots.

He tried not to think about why she'd changed her clothes or the fact that she'd caught him ogling her more than once despite the awful circumstances surrounding them. Hell, he wanted to stare a little longer, memorize every curve of her body and freckle on her nose, but it wasn't time to think about what he wanted. It was time to focus on what Kara needed, which was safe passage out of there with her baby.

He rubbed his neck and forced a casual tone. "Yeah." He took another look at the pink dotted bags. *Casey's* bags. He tried hard to reconcile the fact at hand with his childish dream that one day they'd have reason to meet again and things between them would be okay. That somehow, their previous life together had only been interrupted, not utterly railroaded. Nevertheless, the truth was everywhere. Ryder had spent three years healing, and Kara had spent the time moving on without him.

As she should have.

He dragged his attention from the tiny luggage to Kara. "You're all packed?"

Her eyes had already been on him, watching as he struggled with the reality of her life in progress. "Am I bringing too much?"

Ryder released a windy sigh. "You're a mom."

"Every day."

Ryder's gut clenched. Kara was supposed to have *his* babies. Be *his* wife. Her firsts were supposed to be his as well.

But he'd ruined that. He'd give anything for a do-over with her, setting things right this time, but not at the expense of her happiness, and based on the photographs weighing down every flat surface, of a blissful Kara and her beautiful baby girl, she was happy.

A mix of emotions swam over her face before she turned on her toes and swept past him. She opened a cupboard door and unloaded empty bottles, canisters of formula and boxes of baby cereal into a purple bag on the counter.

A few moments later, she looked up, crossed her arms and stared hard. "I'm going to assume you smell something bad and that ugly frown doesn't have anything to do with me being a mother."

Ryder slid a hand across his forehead, smoothing the angry lines that had gathered there. "No. It looks good on you."

"Sure," she nodded, mocking. "I'm three years older and twenty pounds heavier than the last time you saw me. I haven't slept in four months, and I answered the door in worn-out running gear. Meanwhile you look…" She waved one hand aimlessly before dropping it back to her side. She groaned and went back to packing baby food.

Ryder drifted closer, unable to help himself. "I wasn't kidding or being polite or whatever you think. You really do look amazing."

She turned to face him, squaring her shoulders and locking him in her gaze. Challenging him.

He tugged the ends of blond waves hanging loosely at her elbows. "Your hair's even longer than I remember, thicker. You're tanner. You look happy." The final word nearly choked him. She was happier after three years without him, even after that other loser she'd been with had left her, than she'd been with him.

He dropped his gaze and stepped away, his breath stolen by the sickening thought. Ryder had no business standing so close to her. No right to interject his desires into her perfectly happy life. He'd done a good enough job of screwing things up three years ago. Right now, he needed to focus on keeping her safe and getting his hands on Timothy Sand before he came at her again.

"I sent prints from the matchbook to West for testing, but I'm positive they'll come back as Sand's."

Kara relented her position, deflated, turned back to the purple bag and tugged the zipper across the top. "I've packed enough for Casey and me to be gone a week. Will that be enough?"

Ryder couldn't let it go this time. "You named her Casey," he said, still mystified. "Why?"

"It's a good name."

"It's my middle name," he said.

Kara stared into his eyes again, a long beat of silence stretching between them. "I know."

Dammit. How could he focus on the job when all he could think about was Kara and what her life was like now? What had it been like for her during those three years he'd missed? Had she thought of him? Was that why she named her baby Casey?

He took a step toward her again. "Kara."

She rolled big blue eyes up at him. "I should probably get some sleep."

Ryder leaned forward. "Please wait."

She didn't move.

He leaned closer still, testing the boundary that must be there and inhaling her sweet scent. She looked so comfortable in her pj's, standing with him in their old home. Everything about the moment was so pleasantly normal that he nearly kissed her.

Except she wasn't his to kiss anymore, and nothing about their sudden reunion was normal.

His heart ached as she turned, and he caught her hand in his for one brief squeeze. She'd found happiness without him, and he needed to let her have it.

Find Sand. Go home. That was what he was there for, not to muck up Kara's life any more than he already had. "Good night, Kara."

KARA MOVED SLOWLY up the steps, forcing herself not to look back or run ahead. The grip Ryder Garrett had on her heart, *had always had on her heart*, was unfair, and darn it, she was mad at him for showing up like this and bringing a killer to her doorstep.

But there was no denying the way he looked at her. As if he didn't see how time had changed her, or didn't care.

She slid under her covers and let the memories come. Good ones this time. The sweet press of his mouth on hers. The taste of his lips. *Of his skin*. All the days she'd spent lost in Ryder's blue eyes and the nights she'd spent wrapped in his arms.

Sleep took her fast despite the danger lurking outside, and Kara woke to the sound of Casey's cry at six sharp. She sat upright with a bolt as the night rushed back to her. Her pajamas clung to the sheen of sweat still moist on her skin. Courtesy of falling asleep thinking of Ryder's body on hers. She plucked the soft cotton shirt away from her chest and peeled long strands of hair off her neck, cheeks and shoulders. Kara ran a hand through tangled waves and sighed. She was a mess. *Doesn't matter*, she chided herself. *He's only here to catch his criminal and leave. He didn't come for you.*

Casey cried again, and Kara flung the sheet away from her body. She padded into the nursery and lifted her baby from the crib for a long snuggle. Casey quieted at the first sight of her mama's face. Kara sat in the nearby rocker for several minutes, giving herself time to cool off, then danced Casey back to the master bedroom, where Kara could freshen up before making an appearance downstairs.

She dropped a Tiffany blue sundress over her head and let her hair fall over both shoulders, then followed with mascara and a swipe of lip gloss, plus a good hair brushing. She'd have preferred a shower and shampoo, but Casey's need for breakfast trumped Kara's need to look pretty, so she descended the stairs with Casey in her arms.

Ryder did a double take when she entered the room. He looked ten years younger sitting on her floor in his old basketball shorts and Shadow Point Football T-shirt, surrounded by scattered papers. His ball cap was on backward and one long arm was looped around a bent knee. "Good morning."

Kara smiled. "You look like you're studying for finals. What is all that?"

He hoisted himself off the floor and loped in her direction. "I wish I was still in school. I'd do a lot of things differently."

"Oh, yeah?" She hoped that she was one of those things. That he'd have chosen her over Timothy Sand.

He stopped just inches from her, reaching out to stroke Casey's cheek. "Good morning."

The weight of his presence seemed to press the air from her lungs all over again.

Kara cleared her throat. "Ryder, this is Casey. Casey, Ryder." She angled herself then, giving Ryder a perfect view of her daughter's beautiful face.

"She's gorgeous."

"Yeah."

Ryder lifted pained eyes to Kara. "She looks just like you."

"Thanks." Kara fought a blush, but lost the battle. "Do you want to hold her?"

"No." He leaned away. Panic lifted his brows, and color bled from his cheeks. "I can't. I've never. So, I shouldn't."

Kara stepped closer, pushing Casey in Ryder's direction. "Go on."

"Uh." He cocked his head and shifted his gaze from Casey to Kara and back.

She smiled, watching the gamut of emotions race over his big, strong, US marshal face. "You can do it. She won't bite."

Ryder flicked his attention back to Kara. "You're taunting me."

"Yeah."

A smile twitched on his lips. "If I drop her, it's your fault."

Kara transferred her tiny princess into Ryder's capable arms.

Casey's pink blankie draped over his elbow, and her wide blue eyes focused intently on his.

Ryder's jaw went slack. His lips parted, and his shoulders dropped away from his ears.

Caught in Casey's spell. Her daughter had that effect on people.

"You won't drop her," Kara said. Her heart swelled

with pride at the beautiful little human she'd made, the one she was raising on her own, the one who was all hers. For the tiniest moment, she wondered what it would be like to share her. She lifted her eyes to Ryder, recalling the amazing, funny, loving protector he had once been, and a wave of longing rolled through her, stealing her breath.

"How do you know?" Ryder asked.

Kara righted her thoughts and dropped a kiss against Casey's soft blond curls, then trailed the backs of her fingers over Ryder's stubble-coated cheek. "Because you're a born protector."

RYDER'S CHEST PUFFED with pride and heated with pleasure at Kara's words, *at her touch*. Her stamp of validation made him feel ten feet tall and unstoppable, but the baby in his arms made him feel curiously weak. As if his heart had been exposed and was suddenly, perilously endangered. By everything.

Was that what Kara felt like all the time now? Did caring for a tiny human do this to a person?

He turned his gaze back to Kara with renewed interest and increased respect. He hadn't thought either was possible. Then he remembered the question in need of an immediate answer. He looked into the tiny angel's gaze once more and felt his bones soften. "Casey," he whispered. Kara had named her daughter after him.

Kara returned a moment later carrying a bottle and tiny stuffed doll wearing a yellow raincoat. She gathered the baby into her arms and laid the doll on Casey's belly, then smoothly maneuvered the bottle into her daughter's eager mouth. "What?" she asked, glancing at him as she got situated.

"Why'd you name her Casey? Don't tell me it's a good name again. It's my name. Why?"

Kara returned her attention to the baby in her arms, hungrily gulping her breakfast.

Ryder swallowed hard. "I need to know."

"Being alone and pregnant was tough," she started softly. "I guess you're the strongest person I know and I missed—"

The doorbell rang, interrupting Kara's words, and a fresh blush colored her cheeks.

Ryder grabbed his sidearm from the floor near his paperwork and shot Kara a pointed look. "Hold that thought. And stay back."

Kara hurried into the next room while he checked the window. "It's West." Ryder swung the door wide and welcomed his little brother with a strong hug.

"It's been a long time, Ry," West said, patting Ryder's back and squeezing him hard.

"Indeed."

The men stepped apart and looked one another over with keen eyes.

West rubbed his chin. "It's good to see you, but I wish it wasn't like this."

"That makes three of us." He cast a wayward look over his shoulder in the direction Kara had run.

"How was the reunion?" West asked, his voice low and pointed.

"Better than I'd expected," Ryder admitted. "Her daughter's in danger because of me, and she still let me live."

"She's either the definition of grace under pressure, or she's making plans to turn you over to Sand."

"The definition of grace, huh?" Kara strolled back into view. Her speed increased with each step until she nearly reached a jog. She lashed her free arm around West's neck and kissed his cheek. "I've missed you so much." She stepped back and beamed. "How are you?"

"Good." West's smile was wide and genuine. "Really good."

Kara's smile stretched impossibly wider. "I read all about your wedding in the paper. There were pictures by that local photographer."

"Marissa," West said. "Blake's wife."

Ryder had three brothers. All incurable playboys, and all recently married. Happy as he was for each of them, it hadn't escaped Ryder's mind that *he* was the first to be engaged. *He* was the one never interested in sampling from some bizarre woman-buffet. Ryder had only ever had eyes for one woman, and she was standing before him now, completely unattainable. And that was all on him.

West's gaze slid to the pink bundle in Kara's arms. "Well, hello," he cooed, slipping into a weird-sounding baby voice. "Who is this?"

"This is my daughter, Casey," Kara said.

West tented his brows. "Casey?"

Kara nodded, color staining her cheeks once more. "That's right." She kept her gaze on Casey while West shot Ryder a smug smile.

"May I?" West asked, nodding toward the infant.

"Sure."

Ryder drifted closer to Kara without thinking and set his palm against the small of her back.

She leaned casually into his touch as West pulled Casey into his arms.

"How soon can we move?" Ryder asked. Things had been too quiet for too long, and his gut said it wouldn't last.

"We're ready," West answered. "I've got two deputies waiting out front to escort us to the new location."

Kara set her hand on Ryder's stomach and rested her head against him, either terrified by the reality of being taken into protective custody with her infant or of the monster making the move necessary, Ryder couldn't be sure.

What he did know was that the heat of her gentle touch had burned a hole in his already aching heart. It wasn't a touch between friends. It was intimate and powerful. He jerked his face toward her, peering down as she looked up. And for the breadth of a heartbeat, there was no denying the emotion in those big blues. In the next moment, her attention was on West and Casey. Her hand at her side.

The doorbell rang, and the trio started. The front porch was empty, yet someone pushed the button over and over, rattling Ryder and launching Kara toward West.

"Back door," she said, hurriedly collecting Casey from his arms.

Ryder was already halfway there, gun drawn and motioning West to follow. It could only be Sand. Who else would push the bell maniacally, as if it was tied direct to Ryder's last nerve. Who else would approach the back door, at this very moment, while two deputies sat out front and the county sheriff stood inside.

Ryder's hands ached from the grip on his gun, but that was nothing compared to the invisible vise around his heart. It was infuriating enough that Sand had come to Shadow Point to taunt him and threaten Kara and Casey. Now he had the nerve to walk up to her door and ring the bell that Ryder had once installed? To darken the doorstep of the porch where Ryder had once proposed? Where Kara had said yes?

Hell. No.

The brothers moved into position against the rear wall.

West nodded, then swung the back door wide.

Ryder darted outside. He cleared the porch, the yard and the alley beyond, where Kara stored the trash bins.

"Ry?" Kara's trembling voice pulled him back to her like the snap of an outstretched rubber band.

She stood in the open kitchen doorway, Casey cradled in one arm, a piece of paper shaking in the grip of her free hand.

West met Ryder on the steps, pushing Kara back inside and locking the door behind them.

"What is it?" Ryder eased into her space. He wrapped a protective arm around her and worked to free the paper from her fingers.

"Us," she whispered.

A pair of photos were printed on copy paper. In the first image, Kara held Casey on one hip, and in the second image, Ryder curled Kara against his chest. The look on his face was pained and fiercely protective. The caption scrawled beneath simply said:

What a lovely family you have there, Marshal. Would be a shame to see it all go up in flames.

Chapter Six

The fine hairs along Kara's neck and arms stood at attention as Ryder pulled his SUV away from the curb with her and everything she cared about stuffed inside. He'd practically thrown her and Casey into the back seat the minute he'd seen the photo and read the note. *What a lovely family you have there, Marshal. Would be a shame to see it all go up in flames.* Her teeth chattered despite the sticky hot temperature. She curled her arms across her chest for warmth.

A killer had walked onto her porch and rung her doorbell.

He'd stood outside watching them. Photographing them.

West glanced at Ryder from his position in the passenger seat. "Tech services is working on a current photo of Sand for the media, and they say they will be able to tell which printer printed the photo once they get a look at it."

"Do we care about the printer?" Kara asked, still shocked by the boldness of Timothy Sand. Weren't there more important questions to ask? Like what else Sand had been up to right underneath their noses?

Ryder glanced at her in the rearview mirror. "We can use the information about the printer to help track Sand's steps, and that's a good thing."

Kara certainly hoped so. She wasn't sure her heart could take much more fear and anxiety. Timothy Sand needed to be stopped. Today.

She set one hand on Casey's car seat, then turned her face toward the morning sun. She tried not to think of how dangerous things could get moving forward or about all the things she'd had to leave behind. The hand-me-down rocker where she'd nursed Casey for the first three months. Her grandmother's afghan. The porch swing where Ryder had proposed. She couldn't take it all with her, but everything she left behind was at risk of being burned to the ground, courtesy of Timothy Sand's fixation on hurting Ryder.

Kara watched as each car, street and friendly face flashed by outside the tinted glass. She searched for signs of danger but found only beauty. Growing fields of corn and sunflowers stood tall and proud beside big red barns and small white houses. Distant forest-covered mountains lined the horizon, but sadly, all the beauty in the world couldn't overpower the tumbling sickness of knowing a crazed arsonist was after her.

Beside her, Casey played contentedly with the plastic teething rings hanging from her car seat. For her, this was just another ride in the car. A quick trip to a new place with love and snuggles on the other side.

Meanwhile, Kara's worst nightmare was unfolding.

West caught Kara's eye in the rearview mirror as Ryder hooked a right through the center of town. "You doing okay?"

Considering the facts at hand? "No."

Cole, the youngest Garrett brother and current Cade County deputy, drove behind them in a faded red pickup, trying to look inconspicuous without his cruiser. Unfortunately, three cars tailing one another through Shadow Point at this hour was conspicuous regardless. It was barely after seven, and shops in town wouldn't open for two hours. Sheriff's cruisers or not, their little caravan might as well have been a Fourth of July parade for all the attention it was getting from people walking their dogs, collecting mail from their boxes or rocking on their front porches.

Kara tried to smile at West's reflection, but couldn't manage the task. Her muscles and insides were knotted tight with fear. "Where are we going?" she asked. It hadn't occurred to her to ask before, but suddenly the destination mattered very much. Would they be safe? Would there be neighbors? *Witnesses?* Would there be collateral damage if Sand caught up with them?

She shivered hard at the thought, then rubbed rough hands against the gooseflesh of her arms. Each

Garrett man was a force of nature. If they thought it would take three of them and an extra deputy to get her out of town safely… Timothy Sand must be the devil.

Kara's fingers curled tighter over the side of Casey's car seat. Sand had been close enough to do the same just yesterday. He'd gripped the stroller and looked at her as if she'd made him angry and not the other way around. It had seemed so strange at the time, but now she understood. He was angry. He'd probably hoped to find Ryder with her at the park.

West twisted at the waist and hung an elbow over the seat for a better look at her. "Our granddad's cabin. You know it?"

A rush of heat coursed over her skin and nostalgia kicked around in her stomach. Kara's gaze jumped to the rearview mirror, where it met with Ryder's steely blue eyes. "Yeah," she said as flatly as possible. How could she forget the place? She'd lost her virginity in that cabin.

West turned back with a nod, attention fixed through the window once more. "I always loved it up there, but I haven't made the trip in years."

Ryder followed the other deputy into the parking lot outside the sheriff's department and chose a space around back. "I want to talk with tech services before we leave town. West's working with them to get Sand's photo on the news and in the local papers. I'd like your stamp of approval on the sketch we share."

"Okay," Kara agreed, thankful to be at the sheriff's department where Casey was sure to be safe.

She pulled Casey's car seat out of the vehicle with Casey strapped safely inside and followed West through the open door. Ryder entered last, keeping a close distance. Always protecting. Always watching.

The sheriff's department bustled with noise and energy, conversations and ringing phones. A vast contrast to the near-silent ride over. From her position near the door, Kara could see all six local deputies, plus folks in jackets with white letters spelling *Crime Scene*.

West and Ryder moved into the midst of the action and the other lawmen began to circle up. Only a few people, still talking on their phones, hung back.

"Kara?" Ryder's voice carried over the white noise around them. He waved a hand, summoning her.

The room watched with expectant faces as she carried Casey's car seat closer.

"What do you think of this rendering?" Ryder asked, turning a photo of the man from the park to face her. "This sketch is based off our most recent photos and an age simulation software."

Her heart rate sputtered, then jolted into a sprint at the sight of him. She immediately recalled the determined set of his jaw. The tenor of his voice, and his hand on Casey's stroller. Unable to find her voice again, she nodded to make sure Ryder understood. Even without a clear view of the man's eyes, she'd recognize that long jaw, narrow chin and broad cheekbones anywhere. She'd never forget them for the rest of her life because now she knew he was the man who wanted to take everything from her. All to spite Ryder, a man who didn't love her anymore. Maybe instead of putting Sand's face on the news, they should hold a press conference announcing the three-year-old breakup. Kara wasn't Ryder's wife. Casey wasn't his daughter. They weren't a family. Sand should keep marching, out of Shadow Point, back to Cincinnati, where he could harass whoever Ryder was involved with today instead of haunting his past.

Ryder's frown deepened. He stuffed two fingertips between his lips and whistled loudly enough to call horses from the next county. "Listen up," he announced to the stilling room. "This is Timothy Sand. We want his face on every television station, every local newscast, relevant website and blog. Push it across social media. Get it out there. Offer a reward. Take every resulting call seriously. When something shakes out, get in touch with West or me immediately. I want this whole town looking for him, maybe even all of Cade County."

The room burst back to life. Men and women hurried to their desks and tapped wildly against the screens of their phones.

Kara concentrated on her breathing, forcing back the panic that threatened to pull her apart.

What a lovely family you have there, Marshal.

The killer's words scratched against her mind. *Would be a shame to see it all go up in flames*. He'd tucked the photo neatly into her window frame as if it was a flyer for a new restaurant and not a threat to burn her baby alive.

Kara counted her breaths, deepening the inhalations. She tried to swallow, but her tongue seemed to have doubled in size. Her mouth was dry. Her eyes wet. Her lips quivered. *Keep it together*, she begged internally.

Casey fussed in her seat, no doubt feeling the intensity of the awful day.

Kara unlatched the five-point safety harness and lifted the little girl into her arms. "Hello, pretty," she cooed, nuzzling her daughter with her nose. "I wish I could think of somewhere out of town to send you until this nightmare is over. Someplace safe. With someone I trust."

But the truth of the matter was that when it came to safety and protection, there was no one better than the Garretts, and they were all in Shadow Point. She pressed Casey's head against her shoulder and bounced gently on her toes, hoping to either entertain her so she wouldn't cry or lull her back to sleep. Kara didn't care which. Once again, she felt a debt of gratitude for the busy sheriff's department. The cabin where they were headed was remote and not easy to find, but there was safety in numbers and something to be said about a room full of men and women licensed to carry a gun. *And trained to fire it.* Kara couldn't think of a safer place for Casey.

She jiggled her baby gently and hummed a happy tune. She left the car seat near the far wall of windows and made a loop around the room's edge, watching the familiar and not familiar faces chatter and design plans to accomplish various goals. Contacting local news networks. Spreading the information online. Surveilling her empty home around the clock in the hopes of catching Sand on the property in search of her.

In the moments she dared a look in Ryder's direction, he was always looking back, as if he'd never let her out of his sight. She recalled his vulnerability at her kitchen table the night before, when he'd told her his story about Timothy Sand. Her heart broke all over again for the lives Sand had taken. The families he'd left permanent holes in. For everyone he'd killed and those he'd left behind.

Kara hummed and bounced Casey, but her attempts at comfort were rejected. Instead, the baby squirmed and fussed against Kara's chest. The strange room with all the new noises had to be the cause, but what could Kara do? Certainly not leave. Instead, she shushed her daughter and planted kisses in her hair, singing softly for only her to hear.

They passed Ryder as he spoke with West. Ryder's eyes were alight with hope and his lips were parted in an almost smile. He was impossibly more handsome than she'd remembered. Ryder clapped West on the shoulder, and her heart stuttered.

The sound reverberated off the walls of her mind, slamming her into a memory of those same strong, confident hands on her body. Those hands had taken her places she'd never been before or since, and she longed for one more trip.

"Kara?" Ryder stood before her.

Kara's muscles tensed with humiliation, caught reliving her most intimate memories in such a public place. And under the most awful of circumstances. What was wrong with her?

"You okay?" He tipped forward for a closer look at her burning face. "Can I get you some water?"

"Yes. Water." She adjusted Casey on her hip, trying desperately to collect herself.

Casey complained. A slobber-covered fist cracked against Kara's cheek.

"Yuck." A bubble of laughter lifted from Kara's chest as she wiped Casey's drippy fingers on her sundress and kissed her daughter's chubby cheeks until she squealed with delight.

Ryder returned with a pointed paper cup. "I couldn't find a normal glass."

"Thank you." Kara gulped the icy drink and wished for more. What she needed was a cold shower and plane tickets to someplace Timothy Sand couldn't find her.

Casey whined again.

This time, Ryder reached for her. "May I?"

"Uh."

"You look like you could use a few minutes," he said. "This is a lot to take in, and I managed not to drop her last time, so…"

"Okay."

"If you want to freshen up or get a snack from the break room, there's time. I'd like to hang around long enough to see Sand's photo make it onto the morning news shows before we leave civilization."

The alarm on her face must've been evident because Ryder smiled. "We'll have everything we need. Don't worry. I've done this before." His brow furrowed suddenly, and his comforting smile faded.

It wasn't hard to imagine the guilt he was feeling. He had done this before. As unintentionally three years ago as it was today, Ryder had put Jennifer Sayers and her family in the psychotic path of Timothy Sand.

That family hadn't made it out alive.

Kara handed Casey over. "Thank you. I only need a minute."

Ryder lifted Casey into the air, and she went silent, gaping down at her mother from the space above Ryder's head.

"Careful," Kara urged, slipping against his side to peer up at her baby.

He brought her back to his opposite hip. The mischievous expression on his lips had vanished, replaced by something dark and meaningful. "You're going to be okay," he vowed. "Both of you."

The deep, convincing promise in his voice was enough to weaken her knees. He used to profess his love to her in that voice. Kara's eyes stung with repressed emotion and unshed tears. The stress of the moment had caught up to her fully, and a fearful tremble worked through her limbs. She and her baby were at the sheriff's department, preparing to flee town in an effort not to be killed by a psychopath. The only bright spot in it all was that she got to see Ryder again and that he was well. But what would become of her when he left again? Why did it hurt so much, even three years later, to know his presence wouldn't last? The whirl of emotion got the best of her and a small sound escaped her lips.

Ryder wrapped his free arm around her, strong and steady as ever. "Come here." He curled her against him, cradling Casey on one side and Kara to his chest. "I know you're scared," he said. "What's happening right now is unthinkable, but it won't last. I've got the county's very best on this case. It's going to be okay," he vowed, "and I will get Sand."

Kara lifted her chin for a better look at the man saying exactly the right words for her frightened heart to hear. Ryder's lips were far closer than she'd expected, and her mouth parted instinctively. The room seemed to fade around them as her gaze rose to meet his. She could kiss him. *He would let me*, she thought. The look in his eyes left no room for doubt about that, but what would it mean? Only a knife through her heart when this was over. A moment of comfort today was not worth the inevitable rivers of tears that would be shed later.

She untangled herself from him, dropped her attention to the floor and forced back the flood of waiting tears. "I just need a minute," she said, waving a hand toward the restroom across the way.

Ryder dipped his chin sharply. The arm he'd secured around Kara curled against Casey's back then, letting her walk away. He turned back to the room's center and the bustling lawmen.

Kara started for the ladies' room, but Casey's abandoned car seat caught her eye. Maybe Rainy Rosie would help make her smile.

The doll wasn't in the seat. She checked through the giant hobo bag on her shoulder. No Rosie. She'd surely remembered to bring her, hadn't she?

Kara moved to the window and looked into the lot, trying to focus her thoughts. She'd been so overcome by the need to pack as many memories as she could, in case Timothy Sand decided to burn her house down, that she'd left Rosie on the sofa. She could picture her there now. She felt the wilting drop of her shoulders as she slumped forward, exhausted. Mentally. Physically. Emotionally. Hopefully Rosie would be safe until they returned. Hopefully her home would be safe.

She hung her head and turned for the ladies' room,

where she could cry out her infinite and multiple frustrations in peace.

Two steps later, an earsplitting boom exploded behind her, knocking her from her feet.

The building shook and glass shattered.

People screamed and scattered, running and shouting as a plume of dust rolled through the sheriff's department and debris fell from the ceiling.

Somewhere in the darkness Ryder screamed her name.

Casey released a sharp gut-wrenching wail that tossed Kara onto her feet and in the direction of the sound.

Her lungs filled with dirt as she raced and fumbled blindly through the smoke-filled building. "Casey!" Kara coughed and hacked against her arm, straining to see her daughter in the thick smoky room. "Casey!"

Kara's ears rang, snuffing out the sounds of panic around her and hastening her footfalls in the general direction where Ryder had last been. Casey's cries had ended. Ryder's voice was gone.

Where were they? What had happened? A barrage of awful, deadly images rampaged through Kara's mind as she swatted and kicked her way through the nearly invisible world around her. As she made slow, bumbling progress toward the exit, bodies bumped against one another and rushed blindly, tripping over toppled desk items and sliding in sheets of broken glass.

Outside, the explosions continued. Booming and echoing from every direction.

What the hell was happening?

Her head beat with pain and the steady whooshing in her ears.

"Casey!" The scream seemed to launch from her very soul.

Where had Ryder and her baby gone? Were they rolled in a heap on the floor? Were they one of the things she'd kicked and hobbled over, unseeing? Kara turned in every direction, begging her eyes to reveal Ryder and Casey, but there was just debris, dust and smoke.

When she looked up once more, the crush of escapees had vanished ahead of her, leaving Kara in the broken building alone. She hoped. "Casey! Ryder!" *Please don't be here. Please don't be hurt. Or worse.*

Her gaze lifted to the bright spot several yards away. Sunlight beyond the open door. The place where everyone had filed outside. She needed to get there, find Ryder and her baby or get help to find them inside the building.

Kara stopped as the deep guttural groan of bending metal rumbled her bones and turned her eyes upward. A series of clicks and snaps echoed overhead, and a portion of the ceiling gave way with a resounding, thunderous crack.

The scream in her throat was extinguished as her body crumbled, crushed beneath an excruciating weight. Kara's world dimmed to black as she sent up a final fervent prayer that somehow Casey had gotten out of this alive. That somehow Ryder had protected her baby.

Chapter Seven

Strong hands wrapped Kara's biceps, pulling her onto her feet. "Can you walk?" Ryder's voice cut through the ringing in her ears. "I can carry you."

She shook her hazy head and shuffled along beside him through piles of plaster and insulation at her feet. "What happened?" she croaked, keenly aware of pain raging in her skull.

The sheriff's department was in utter disarray. The front windows were broken, and shards of glass cluttered the floor. A giant dust cloud loomed in the air, thinner now, but evoked memories of the explosion. She'd been looking out the window near Casey's car seat. Rainy Rosie was missing. Then, she'd turned away toward the ladies' room.

"Casey!" She pulled against Ryder's hand, scanning the floor in a frenzied panic. Her baby had been in his arms when the blast went off, but where was she now? Why wasn't Ryder looking for her? "Casey!" Fire scorched up Kara's windpipe, morphing her screams into deep, throaty hacks. Her eyes and nose burned from smoke still trapped in her throat and lungs.

"She's okay." Ryder struggled to find a new hold on Kara's squirming arms. "She's with West. She's fine. He's fine. I went to find you. He took her outside."

"Where?" She coughed, straining to see West in the mass of distant bodies lining the parking lot. "Where?" she repeated, forcing more demand into her quavering voice.

"There." He extended an arm to the thickest part of the grouping.

Kara squinted against the blast of sunlight as they stepped through the door and into the parking lot. "I don't see her."

"Cole," Ryder barked. He waved a hand overhead, and his youngest brother lifted his chin in acknowledgment. Cole had gone to medical school before deciding to be a lawman. She still had trouble understanding why. All Ryder had to say about it when they were together was that the law was in the Garrett blood. "Over here."

Ryder set his hands on her cheeks, gently bringing her gaze to his. "Look for his hat. West is getting things back in order. Casey is with him. You need to stay here while Cole looks you over." He cupped her face in his palms, leveling her with a heartbroken stare. "Casey's fine." His voice was low and careful. "We weren't near any of the blasts. Nod if you understand."

Kara blinked through tears of relief, praying his words were true and needing to see for herself that they were. Where her baby was concerned, she wouldn't take chances.

Ryder released her. He lifted a finger toward the people once more.

This time, Kara looked for the broad brimmed sheriff's hat, its peak standing just above the crowd. A moment later, the group shifted, parting and reassembling into smaller factions, revealing Casey on West's hip. He gave orders to the deputies and other bystanders, motioning with his free hand, holding Casey in place with the other. As if it was perfectly normal to run the show with an infant attached to his side.

Her pulse lowered a bit. "Okay." She nodded, and pain split the top of her head. Casey was okay, but Kara definitely wasn't. "I think the ceiling fell on me."

"Drywall," Ryder said, looking half ill. "The blast shook the building and an older section of the ceiling gave way." He rubbed his forehead with force. "I thought you were dead."

Kara lifted careful fingers to her scalp and the warmth of fresh blood coated her fingertips. "I'm not dead." She stepped away, but Ryder caught her again. This time, she shot him a warning look. "I want to see her, Ryder. Let go."

"Cole!" Ryder yelled, authority tightening the word. "Get over here."

Kara took another step and his grip tightened. "I will take you with me," she threatened.

Ryder released her, lifting open palms into the air. "She's fine. You're not. You need to stay here and let Cole look at you. You were just in an explosion," he nearly shouted.

"So was she!"

A few faces turned in Kara's direction.

She didn't care.

"Your hair has blood and dirt streaked through it," Ryder snapped. "Your face is scratched up and filthy. At least take five minutes to get your bearings before you march over there and collapse or something."

Kara glanced down at herself. She was a mess. He wasn't lying. The blood on her fingertips came into view then. She swept her attention back to Casey on West's hip. She wanted to hold her, kiss her, tell her everything was okay.

"Five minutes," Ryder asked.

She swung her gaze to him. "What happened in there?"

Ryder's expression was remorseful. He was making her mad, but she could see the regret in his eyes. He blamed himself for what had happened.

What *had* happened?

"You were near the window." He locked his jaw and lifted his gaze over her shoulder.

Cole Garrett jogged swiftly in her direction, toting a red tackle box with a white cross on top. Behind him, and all around the building, dumpsters roared in flames. The largest fire was just outside the window where she'd been standing.

A sob broke in her throat, and she wrapped her arms around Ryder's sturdy core.

He closed his arms over her and held her tight.

Kara's will to be strong faltered in his embrace. She'd grown tougher in his absence and had eventually become Casey's refuge, but in that moment, her strength was testing its limits. Ryder's arms had once been her safe haven. A place where she could be vulnerable. Somewhere harm couldn't find her. And she needed that now more than ever.

The wailing cry of emergency vehicles broke into her awareness.

Kara pulled back with a start, remembering how many people had been inside when the explosion occurred. "Is anyone hurt?"

"You," Cole said, flashing a light into her eyes. "Everyone else was in an office or gathered with Ryder by the far wall, going over strategy protocols and sorting details for the news reports."

"Was it Sand?" she croaked.

Ryder's Adam's apple bobbed long and slow, but he didn't answer. The look on his face said it all. *This was Sand.* And that alone said so much more.

RYDER KEPT AN eye on Kara as a line of unnecessary ambulances roared to a stop in the parking lot and along the street. Despite the extensive property damage, the only person in need of medical attention was Kara, and she could barely hold still while Cole checked the gash on her head and tested her for a concussion.

The fire trucks arrived next, spilling men in traditional yellow gear onto the pavement.

Uncle Henry was the first EMT to make his way from the bus to Ryder's side. The others went to check the unharmed crowd.

"Everyone's okay," Cole said, addressing Henry as he crossed the final few yards between them. "Except this one." He dabbed an alcohol-soaked pad against her head, and she winced. "She's going to need stitches."

Kara shot Cole a threatening look. "I need to see my daughter."

"Take it easy," Cole said, his face sliding from all-business to slightly playful. "I'll send big brother this way. She's all yours Uncle Henry. Strap an oxygen mask over her mouth, would ya?"

Ryder bristled and fought the urge to trip his cocky brother before he said anything so curt to her again. Cole and Kara had always had a playful banter, but this wasn't the time for it, and it wasn't fair that Cole could fall back into step with her so easily after so long. He settled for glaring as Cole walked away.

Henry greeted Kara with a warm hug, then quickly got to work. To Kara's apparent dismay, he took Cole's advice and snapped an oxygen mask over her face. "This will help with the breathing. You probably took in a lot of smoke and dirt. Were you un-conscious at any point?"

"Yes," Kara answered with a deep inhalation, seeming suddenly thankful for the cumbersome mask.

Henry opened his medical kit. "How long was she out, Ryder?"

"Two minutes. Maybe less. I saw her go down, then I passed her baby off to West and shoved them out the door. I went to her from there. Took thirty seconds to pull the drywall away. She was out when I got ahold of her." Two minutes. The words sounded insignificant, but it was the length of two lifetimes. Pulling the drywall away and not knowing what he'd find beneath had been the worst moments of his life. He'd imagined the worst. The bloody, gory, irrepa-rable worst. He rubbed the spot on his chest where it ached with fear again at the memory.

Henry gave her a careful exam, then cleaned and sutured her head. The cut wasn't as bad as all the blood had made it seem. She was finished after only two stitches.

Kara tried to leave again, but Henry held her fast.

"Almost done," he'd promised multiple times, ex-amining every infinitesimal cut and bruise he could find. Several minutes passed before he relented his cause. "I think that'll do it. Come see me if you feel nauseous, light-headed or get any double vision." He handed Kara a two-pack of pain relievers, then cracked open a small bottle of water for her.

Satisfied, he slid smoothly from medic to uncle mode, swinging his face to Ryder. "What the hell happened here?"

"Arson."

He nearly laughed at the ridiculous answer. *Arson.* The word was far too tiny to describe the destruction and chaos swirling around them now. A sheriff's department temporarily out of service. Firefighters circling the building. Every deputy and the sheriff of Cade County displaced into a parking lot surrounded by local onlookers wondering what on earth had happened in their quiet little town.

Kara seized her moment and stripped the oxygen mask off her head. "Thank you." She handed it back to Henry. "I'm going to check on Casey."

Ryder trailed behind her, waving his uncle off. His brothers could fill Uncle Henry in on the details, whatever they turned out to be. He wasn't letting Kara out of his sight again. The moment he'd turned his back on her inside, all hell had broken lose.

Kara kicked into a sloppy jog as she neared West and her baby girl. A tear rolled over her cheek, glistening in the sunlight. "Casey," she cooed. "Come here, sugar." She scooped the little nugget off West's hip and hugged her tight.

West tipped his head, urging Ryder closer. A fireman stood with a clipboard and grimace before him. "Chief Michaels was going over some preliminary findings. You want to jump in on this?"

Kara moved into position at West's side, as if West had been speaking to her.

Ryder fought the quirk of his lips. "What do you know?" He crossed his arms to keep his hands off Kara, and focused on the fire chief.

The chief looked at his clipboard. "The fires in the dumpsters were primed with kindling and ignited with Molotov cocktails. The receptacles closest to the building also had M-80s inside. Those were the blasts that continued after the initial eruption."

"All of the dumpsters?" Kara asked, drawing the chief's attention. "Could one man have done this on his own?"

An excellent question. Ryder looked to the chief, his gut twisting at the thought of someone like Sand with an accomplice.

"If it was well planned, maybe even rehearsed, yes. But for one man to pull this off, the execution would have had to be perfect."

Ryder groaned. Perfectionism was one of Sand's more infuriating qualities. It was nearly impossible to get ahead of a criminal who planned ahead and had contingencies in place for everything. He shuddered as sickness coiled through his gut at the thought of other potential traps Sand might have set in other locations where he suspected Ryder might take Kara. "We need to be on the lookout for other setups like this. He didn't have time to do this while we were in the building. He must've set up sometime earlier and waited for us to show up in the blast range. There could be more like this all over town."

West and the chief nodded. Ryder could count on them to send search teams into the community.

Meanwhile, Ryder scanned the fringe for signs of his nemesis. He needed a watertight plan to get Kara and her daughter to safety without Sand seeing. It wouldn't be easy. Ryder could practically feel Sand's menacing eyes on them now. He repositioned himself at Kara's back and placed a hand on her shoulder. He needed to move her before something else exploded.

Kara or her daughter might not be so lucky the next time.

Chapter Eight

Ryder took advantage of the chaos before it settled and loaded Kara into the back of a panel van driven by the crime scene crew. Cole tagged along just in case.

They waited there, unseen for nearly an hour before the van pulled away with a number of other vehicles. *If Sand was watching. If he'd noticed they were missing.* He'd be hard pressed to guess where they'd gone, and he couldn't follow every exiting vehicle at once.

Ryder made a show of leaving alone, followed by West in the sheriff's cruiser. They needed to examine the perimeter of Kara's home. They knew Sand had been there this morning, at least long enough to take the picture he'd left for them on her kitchen window, and he wasn't a ghost, so he had to have left trace evidence of some kind. Footprints. Fingerprints. *Something.* At least, that was Ryder's prayer as he drove slowly back through town. They would also search for more of Sand's little booby traps. More fires waiting to happen.

Ryder checked the clock on his dashboard, already wishing he was back with Kara and her baby.

If all went as planned, the ladies would be at his mom and dad's home in time for dinner. It would make for a long day, but at least it would be a safe one. Ryder had sent Kara and her daughter back to the crime scene offices in the panel van, where they would pass the time until the workday ended, then they would ride in a crime scene team member's SUV to the Garrett homestead, which was on one guy's way home. Anyone watching would see nothing unusual, except the pit stop to deliver the women. Then again, Sand would never see that stop because the Garretts lived on a narrow country road that would make it impossible for anyone to tail the SUV. If the SUV's driver suspected someone was following him, he would go on to the Cade County jail, where a solitary confinement cell would be waiting to protect Kara and Casey until Ryder could arrive, corner and capture their stalker. If Sand was brave and stupid enough to try an ambush, he'd meet the business end of a department-issued Glock.

A few minutes later, West rocked his cruiser to a stop in Kara's drive and lumbered out.

Ryder followed suit. He gave the home a long appreciative look by the light of day before joining his brother on the little walkway to the only window where the photo could have been taken. Flower beds lined the walk and rosebushes flanked the porch. A small, hand-painted sign hung between two red rockers beside the door, with the words *Life is better on the porch* painted in Kara's curly script. A tall, narrow sign beside the steps read *WELCOME* in big block letters. His finger curled at his sides as he moved into place outside the window where Sand had stood watching them. Trees and thick masses of red roses obstructed the view from anywhere besides that specific space on the walkway. Sand had been right there, separated from Ryder by a thin pane of glass, and Ryder had had no idea.

West dropped into a squat, scanning the ground for clues. "Don't look so grim, brother."

Ryder responded with a scoff, trailing his gaze over the blooming flower bed and tidy cobblestones. "I'm not sure how else to look right now."

West stretched back to his full height and clapped him on the back. "It's not over yet."

"Damn right." He shook his head in disgust. "This won't be over until Sand is behind bars where he can't hurt anyone else ever again."

West narrowed sharp eyes on Ryder and smiled. "We both know that's not what I meant."

Ryder's gut gave a squeeze, and he turned away. A future with Kara Noble and her sweet baby girl wasn't in the cards for him. The best he could hope for now was nailing Sand to the wall like he should've before, and if he was really lucky, Kara might someday forgive him for all the trouble he'd caused her.

KARA HELD FAST to Casey as the SUV clamored to a stop behind the Garrett homestead.

Mr. Garrett greeted Kara's driver, shotgun in hand. Square-jawed and ruggedly handsome like his sons, the retired sheriff was a patriot and born protector. Her heart kicked at the sight of him. To know Mr. Garrett was to understand his boys. Their instinctual and profound quests for justice were the stuff of storybooks. *Unfortunately*, Kara thought, recalling the awful stories Ryder had shared with her about the murders Sand had committed while Ryder had been in pursuit of him, *not every fairy tale has a happy ending.*

Cole climbed down to talk with his dad.

Kara opened her door and stepped into the sunlight, examining the beauty around her. The intoxicating scents of fresh-cut grass, hay and horses rushed up to greet her. The Garrett farm was gorgeous, well loved and frequented by a large and proud family. Memories of backyard barbecues, birthdays and holidays around the gathering-room fireplace raced into mind. If breaking up with Ryder had been the hardest thing she'd ever done, then cutting ties with his family had been a close second.

The back door opened and Mrs. Garrett barreled out. Her graying hair was swept into a bun, and flyaway strands fluttered at her temples as she made a run for Kara, arms wide. "Baby girl," she cooed, wrapping her in a warm embrace. In that moment, in her arms, Kara was safe. The world was as it should be. And Ryder was inside, setting their plans for an evening of handholding and kissing under the stars.

Mrs. Garrett kissed Kara's cheeks and stroked Casey's soft curls. "I'm so glad you're home."

Emotion clogged Kara's throat as the weight of the day nearly overcame her once more. "Thank you for having me," she whispered, not trusting her voice to be any louder without cracking.

Mrs. Garrett released her and reality returned with a smack. A chill rushed against Kara's chest in her absence, despite the blazing summer temperatures.

She couldn't help wondering if this would've been her life sooner if she'd have married Ryder. Aside from the shotgun at his hip, Mr. Garrett seemed completely at ease, as if this was just another day in the life of a lawman. Was this what Mrs. Garrett's life had been like for twenty years while her husband was the local sheriff? Was this what Ryder's brothers' wives went through? Weekly? Daily? How could they do it?

Casey wriggled in her arms, letting out a soft warning. She was tired, overstimulated, ready for a bottle and probably needed a dry diaper.

"It's okay," Kara cooed.

Casey blinked. Her fussing stilled and a warm, toothless smile broke over her face.

And then she knew. The women in the Garrett men's lives did whatever it took because they loved them. Kara would do anything for Casey. Even trade her life to protect her daughter's. That was the kind of love the Garrett men had found, and as unreasonable as it was for Kara to think so, she was sure Ryder would do the same for her. Regardless of the wreck their relationship had become and all the time that had been lost between them.

"This way." Mrs. Garrett turned her toward the house by her shoulders. "Let's go inside and get all caught up now. I've already put on a roast, potatoes, carrots and fixed a salad. And there's sweet tea on the counter."

"You shouldn't have," Kara said, settling into step at her side.

"Nonsense. It's been too long for you and me, and you've got someone here to introduce me to." She pulled the back door open and smiled at the sleepy baby in Kara's arms. "Who is this?"

"Casey." Kara managed to maintain eye contact with Ryder's mother, despite the obvious desperation in that word. How sad was it that she'd named her child after the ex she'd never stopped pining for?

Mrs. Garrett gave a knowing smile. "Seems we have more to talk about than I thought."

The sound of crunching gravel stopped their progress. A vehicle was approaching on the long, winding drive, and Kara's muscles went rigid with fear as she waited for it to roll into sight.

Before she had a good view, Mr. Garrett waved a hand overhead and smiled.

Her shoulders relaxed. Mr. Garrett knew the visitor. She was safe.

Mrs. Garrett bounced on her toes as Ryder's truck

rolled to a stop beside the family home. She clapped her hands and darted back off the porch and across the lawn toward her son.

The driver of the SUV Kara had arrived in shook Mr. Garrett's hand, then climbed back into his truck. Cole hugged his dad, saluted Ryder's truck, then joined the crime scene guy on a return trip down the lane. Kara lifted a hand to wave goodbye. She'd forgotten to thank them for her safe passage.

Ryder and his parents joined her on the porch and ushered her inside.

The cozy kitchen smelled like brown gravy, apple pie and brewing coffee. The scents wafted tantalizingly through the air, resurrecting a forgotten hunger in Kara's empty belly. She hadn't eaten today, and while she knew she should have, fear had made it impossible. The most she'd managed to consume at the crime scene department was some orange juice while she cleaned up her face and hair. She'd need a shower and shampoo to get all the bits of drywall debris from the strands.

Ryder poured Kara a cup of coffee, then took the seat beside her. His hair was disheveled, as if he'd run his fingers through it too many times, and there was weariness in his eyes. Something hadn't gone as planned at her house. She could only hope it was still standing and not in a pile of ashes.

"Thanks." She wasn't ready to ask.

He examined her and Casey with careful eyes. "You okay?"

"Yeah."

Mrs. Garrett dragged a high chair to the island and pulled Casey from Kara's arms. "I'll take this one," she said, giving the baby a little wiggle. "Well, hello, Casey!" She made a silly face, then kissed her chubby cheeks and deposited her into the seat. "I told West that I was smart to buy baby things for my house," she said to Casey in a high-pitched voice. She fished infant toys from a quilted bag hanging on the back of the high chair. "Every good and decent grandma has her own baby things." She lined bulbous plastic farm animals on the tray for Casey to chew or knock down.

"Grandma Garrett had a farm," she sang, "E-I-E-I-O."

"She hates being a grandma," her husband deadpanned.

Kara smiled, warmth blooming in her chest. "I see that." Kara's parents hadn't seen Casey since her delivery, and while she hoped to travel to Oregon to see them for the holidays, that was a long time from now, and Casey wouldn't know them then. The idea of having a local grandma like Kara had had was heartwarming. Some of her very best memories were made at her grandma's side.

She blew across the bitter tendrils of steam rising from her cup, gathering her courage before forcing the nagging question from her lips. "How'd it go at my place?" She braced herself, half afraid to know the answer.

He gave his head a firm shake. "Nothing."

Kara nodded. They were no closer to catching Sand now than they were yesterday when they didn't even know he was in town.

Mr. Garrett leaned his elbows on the island. "Care to fill me in on why this is happening? I got the wiki version from your brothers, and I already know all about Sand. What I don't understand is what he's doing here."

Ryder rocked onto one hip and removed a wallet from his back pocket. He slid a folded newspaper article from beneath a leather flap. "I attend the Sayers Vigil in Ohio every year. Jennifer's family invites everyone to the town square. Folks who knew her or her children share stories about them. Others take the podium as experts on the topics of stalking, domestic violence and mental health awareness." He slid the newspaper to his dad. Red ink circled part of the crowd. "This year, I thought I saw Sand there."

Kara moved to stand behind Mr. Garrett. She examined the grainy image over his shoulder. "I can't tell if that's him."

"It's him," Ryder said. "I wasn't sure at the time, but I know it now. The image was taken from quite a distance, and it's grainy, but I was there." He tapped a finger just outside the photo. "I tried to find him in the crowd, but he'd disappeared. I thought it was my imagination. That somehow being there, in that town, seeing photos of the lost family had conjured old ghosts. Until West called last night to tell me what had happened to you. It didn't make sense for Sand to risk attending the Sayerses' vigil."

Mr. Garrett gave a sad smile. "He wasn't there for them, Ry. He was there for you."

RYDER CARRIED HIS dad's words with him throughout the evening, running all over town with West and two marshals who'd come to help locate Sand. As usual, the efforts were futile, and Ryder returned to his parents' home with no news to share.

If there was a bright side to an otherwise terrible day, it was that the sheriff's department had cleaned up well. The windows had been replaced, and an electrician had deemed the facility safe for business. The drywaller couldn't repair the ceiling until Monday, but that didn't matter. Everyone was back in their places and working hard to find Sand before he could do any more damage to their town.

His chest tightened at the sight of Kara and his mother on the old porch swing. Casey was fast asleep in Kara's arms.

Ryder climbed the steps slowly, taking in the lovely view. "Evening, ladies." He kissed his mom's cheek and stroked the fluffy yellow curls on Casey's head. "How are y'all holding up?"

His mom rose to hug him around the neck. "We're just fine, but it looks like you could use some rest." She turned to face Kara. "How about I put on some hot tea and take this little one off your hands so the grown-ups can talk?"

Kara's gaze jumped from Ryder to his mother. "Oh, no. You don't have to. She'll wake and fuss. You're already doing too much."

"Nonsense," Mrs. Garrett reached for the baby. "She can sleep in the nursery where all my grand-babies stay when they visit."

Kara flushed.

His mom must've read the emotion on her face because she leaned forward, cuddling Casey to her chest and whispered, "You'll always be part of this family. Your little one, too." With that, she carried Casey inside, leaving Kara and Ryder alone on the dark porch.

He lowered himself onto the swing beside Kara. "She's right, you know? They're still your family. They adopted you the moment you showed up for dinner with me five years ago."

"I've missed them," she said.

Ryder considered his response. He could stay focused on the case, or he could make sure Kara knew she was his top priority, like he should have before. "I've missed *you*," he said finally.

She swung her face away from him.

Three years too late, he thought as she wrapped

her arms around her middle. He was too late, but at least he'd finally told her.

She flicked an uncharacteristically shy look in his direction. "I've missed you, too," she said. "Every day."

Ryder's jaw sank open. "What?" He stared hard into her big blue eyes, willing her to say it one more time.

"Every day."

His arms were around her then, pulling her close. He buried his face in her hair and inhaled the sweet scent of her. The thrill of his heart pounding against hers enveloped him, and when he thought he couldn't take any more, she hugged him back.

Not just a hug. Kara melted into him. "I'm scared, Ryder."

"I know," he whispered, "but you don't have to be. Sand is on his way out of Shadow Point, and I'm going to be his escort." He brushed soft hair off her shoulder, wishing the moment could last, and that Timothy Sand's wretched name wasn't part of it.

She wiggled her head against his chest, peering up at him in the night. "Are we putting your family at risk by staying here?"

"No." Ryder cleared his throat. "When you're here, Dad's on duty. Every Garrett has gone all-in on this case, from Dad and me to West and Cole, even Blake." His oldest brother, Blake, was a federal agent living in town, and Blake liked nothing better than capturing guys like Sand. "Plus, there are two more marshals in town now," he added. "They trailed Sand to a fleabag hotel on the outskirts of town before he vanished. He'll be too busy staying clear of them to find you tonight."

Kara shifted positions on the swing, releasing his torso and tucking her feet beneath her on the soft cushion. She leaned her weight against his side, setting her gaze on the horizon.

Ryder planted his boots against the floor and swung them gently, absorbing the moment, with its lilac-scented air, bullfrog-and-cricket chorus and firefly light show. "You know," he said, unwilling to miss another opportunity to say the things that had weighed on him for so long. "I was wrong to lose myself in the work like I did. I was too young and too green to know it would swallow me whole if I let it. You didn't deserve that."

"Can I ask you something?" she said, her voice more timid than he'd heard it before.

"Anything." His nerves bundled as he waited. Would she want to know why he'd chosen chasing Sand over being her husband? Why he'd given up a future with her to follow a psychopath? Because no answer would ever be good enough. And there was no sense to be made of it.

"Are you disappointed in me?" she asked.

"What?" He cocked his head back for a look into her eyes, but she kept her attention on the distant field. "Why would I be?"

"Oh, I don't know." She sighed. "Maybe for letting a man into my life who I knew wasn't the one my heart truly wanted. It sounds dumb, but I feel like I let you down that way. I was selfishly trying to fill the void you'd left, and I should've known no one else could."

Ryder bristled. "I could never be disappointed in you," he said, mad all over again at the moron who'd left her and Casey to figure things out on their own. "What were you supposed to do? Your fiancé lost his damn mind and moved out to chase a killer. Your wedding was canceled. Your world changed irreparably because of me. I'd never blame you for anything you did to get through that."

An ugly thought wound through his mind then, and the words were on his lips in seconds. "But I am jealous. I've got no right to be, but I am."

"Of what?" She turned to him with a frown that seemed to say he was crazy for being jealous.

"Of knowing you found love somewhere else," he said. "Knowing you let another man into your heart…" *Into your bed.* "I thought you'd gotten married, had a baby, done all the things we'd planned to do together, with someone else…" *A jerk who'd walked away.* He grimaced, feeling the unreasonable clench of his jaw. "You had every right, and I have no business saying so, but I hate that guy."

Kara laughed, her expression moving swiftly to something light and peaceful.

Ryder scanned her curiously. He'd expected her to read him his rights.

"I kind of hate that guy, too," she said. "But the truth is nothing has ever felt right since you left." A tear fell onto her cheek, and Ryder wiped it away. "I had to let you go because you'd chosen the hunt over me. Over us."

The words were a punch to his gut, but he deserved that.

"It feels like the worst days of my life are happening all over again," she said, "except this time everything's worse. This time my baby and I are in danger while you're hunting this lunatic."

"It's not like that," Ryder said, reaching for her hand. "I'm not the same man I was then, and I wouldn't even be chasing Sand right now if he hadn't come for you."

A fat tear rolled onto Kara's cheek. "Why'd you do it before?"

Ryder hung his head, feeling the leaden weight of her question on his shoulders. There was no good answer for what he'd done or for the pain he'd caused. Youthful ignorance seemed like an excuse, but that was what it had boiled down to. "I thought catching Sand would prove something. Make me a better man. A stronger protector. Save the world." He gave a low and humorless laugh. "I reached rock bottom that first year without you, and it took a while, but I got help, turned myself around and made Sand a side project instead of my purpose in life. I even turned the case over to a colleague while I left town to relocate a family in WitSec. Sand burned down another home while I was gone. My stupid colleague presented a case weaker than Grandma's coffee, and Sand got off with a scolding and some probation. Now, he's free again and here we are."

"Your dad's right, then. He's come for you," she said.

Ryder gave a sad smile. "Yeah." He set a hand along her jaw, curling his fingers against her warm skin. "I swear I never dreamed he'd go after you. I had no idea he knew you existed."

"I know."

"It doesn't make sense for him to go after the woman who kicked me out of her life. He has to know by now. He seems to know everything."

"Maybe he just wanted to go back to where it all started with you?" Kara offered.

"Maybe." Ryder felt his brows furrow. Everything that had mattered in his adult life had started with Kara, and he wanted her at his side for everything else that mattered, too, but how could he ask her for anything when he'd ruined what they'd had in the past. And he was still hurting her now?

"I will fix this," he said, wishing she could see it was true. "I won't let Sand get near you, and I swear I will never do anything to hurt you again."

Kara's emotion-filled gaze slipped from his eyes to his lips. "Promise me," she said, curving feather-light fingers against the back of his head and pulling him nearer.

"I promise," he vowed.

Then, he covered her mouth with his.

Chapter Nine

Ryder's cell phone interrupted the moment he'd been waiting impatiently for these last three years. He pulled back, apologetically, taking his time to remove his hands from Kara's perfect cheeks. "Don't move."

Kara blushed, but nodded.

His heart hammered as he dug his phone from his pocket, cursing whoever had ruined the moment. West's face glowed across the screen. "This had better be good, brother," Ryder said.

"I know you've been at it all day," West began, "but I need boots on the ground near the old bank building, and frankly, we're running low on boots."

Ryder heard him out and stuffed the phone back into his pocket.

"What?" Kara asked, already on edge. "Did something else happen?"

"No, but I've got to go." He heaved a long breath and dragged one palm over his face. This was exactly the kind of thing that had broken them up before. "The barista at the coffee shop across from the sheriff's department made a call to dispatch on her way home a few minutes ago. She said there was a man at the coffee shop when the fires broke out earlier, and he stuck by the windows watching the fallout to the very end. She didn't get a good look at his face, but she saw the car he got into when he left. She just saw that car again parked alone in an alley down by the bank."

"You think Sand is at the bank?" Kara asked. "Why?"

"It's probably nothing." Ryder reached for her hand and cupped it in his. "No one was in the car, and we don't know it was Sand she saw earlier. Someone still needs to check it out. Run the plates. See who it belongs to."

Kara nodded. "Okay. I'll come with you."

"I don't think so."

"Why? You said you're just going to call in the plate number, and we still have plenty to talk about, like how long Casey and I are supposed to hide from Sand while you hunt him down and bring him in."

Ryder considered her request. In any other circumstance, he would've said absolutely not, but this seemed like a good opportunity to show her he really had changed. He could go check out a car's plate without spending the night on the streets searching for Timothy Sand. And to be honest, he wasn't ready to say goodbye again.

Kara watched him. Her lips pressed into a thin line.

"Okay." Ryder pushed onto his feet and extended

a hand. "Come on, then. Let's get this done so we can come home and kiss good-night."

THE DRIVE TO the bank was short. Kara had been quiet, but his phone had been busy. Cole was en route to the bank, but he was still ten minutes out. Everyone else was tied up, already chasing tips and leads that had come in following the evening newscast.

"Look," Kara said. "There."

The barista had been right. There was a car in the alley beside the bank, but Sand wasn't a bank robber, so Ryder wasn't concerned. He radioed the plate in to dispatch and turned back to Kara. "See? Easy."

She was pale in the moonlight streaming through the windshield. "What if this is an ambush?"

Ryder shook his head. "He has no idea the barista noticed him earlier, or that she saw the car he got into, or that she drives past the bank on her way home. Wait here while I peek in the windows. Due diligence," he explained, "then let's get out of here." He lifted her hand to his lips and left a kiss there before climbing out from behind the wheel.

Ryder shut Kara inside the truck, then went in for a closer look at the car. It was locked. No one inside. Nothing notable on the seats.

"Ry?" Kara called. Her voice carried through his windshield in the silent alley. She pointed toward the brick building opposite the bank.

Ryder followed her troubled gaze to a rear entrance. He crossed the alley for a better look at the door in question.

He swore under his breath. The door was ajar.

Behind him, the soft snick of his closing truck door drew his attention to Kara, hurrying across the alley to his side. "Are you going in there?"

"You're supposed to stay in the tuck." He scanned the alley before sending texts to West and Cole. "Cole will be here any minute," he told her, reading their responses aloud. "West is contacting the store manager." He squinted at the next incoming message from West, then backed up to stare at the darkened building. "This is a camping store?"

"Yeah," Kara whispered, a quiver in her voice. "The drugstore closed last year."

Tension knotted in Ryder's gut. It couldn't be a coincidence that he'd wound up there while following a lead on Sand.

Kara shivered at his side, one small hand wrapped around his elbow. "What should we do?"

"We should wait in the truck until Cole gets here."

Kara's safety was Ryder's top priority. He pressed a hand against her back and forced his feet away from the store.

They'd barely taken a full step before a harrowing thud echoed through the partially open door, followed by a series of muffled grunts and ugly, strangled sounds.

Kara gasped. Her wide, questioning eyes turned to Ryder.

"Get in the car," he told Kara. "Lock the doors." He removed his gun from the holster. "I need to make sure no one is hurt."

Kara shook her head. "No way."

"Go," Ryder demanded, lowering his voice. "Cole is on his way. I need to be sure the building is clear and some poor stock boy isn't in danger."

"No," she repeated. "The man who wants to kill me is probably in there, and you want me to wait alone in a dark alley while you go inside? What if he slips out another exit and comes for me?"

Ryder ground his teeth. Kara was right, but if someone was hurt inside the building, he couldn't walk away. He also couldn't leave her alone in the alley. *Where the hell was Cole?*

The guttural scream of a man in pain split the air and stood the hair on Ryder's arms at attention. He sent one more text, this time to dispatch, requesting an ambulance, then turned to Kara. "Stay close."

She gripped the material of his shirt and moved in close to his back.

Ryder pulled the door open, senses on high alert.

Inside, security lighting glowed eerily over the store's central merchandise, casting heavy shadows over the perimeter and much of the store. Large taxidermy displays of mounted animals loomed around them and looked down from balconies, making it seem like a hundred glass eyes were watching. The choking sounds of distress came again, and Kara's fingers tightened in the material of his shirt.

Ryder moved swiftly through the darkened racks of clothing and camping gear, toward a massive hunting knife display, wishing for all the world he'd left Kara at home. He didn't want to think about the reason a man like Sand would break into a store like this or what he'd find on the other side of the ghastly noises.

There were too many places to hide. Too many unknowns, and yet what could he do besides hope whoever he heard struggling for air would survive whatever Sand had likely done to him or her?

Ryder stopped short as the outline of a man's broad shoulders came into view. Only a tall narrow display of designer oars stood between them.

Ryder raised a palm, signaling Kara to slow, then directing her, silently, to wait as he continued on. With Kara safely tucked into the shadow of the wall, Ryder aimed his weapon. "US marshal. Hands where I can see them."

The figure raised both palms. The strangled gurgling sound came again. Louder now.

Instinct moved Ryder more quickly toward the man. Something was wrong. This wasn't Sand. Sand never would've obeyed so easily. *Unless this was a trap.* He lowered his gun, shocked as the silhouette came clearly into view. The man seemed to be tied upright with a hammock fixed tightly around his torso and the oar display. Ryder hustled closer, and the man's bloodied face and throat came into view. His uniform identified him as the night watchman.

His eyes were wide with panic, held open by adrenaline and fear. Blood rolled in steady lines around the metal of a serrated hunting blade shoved through the side of his throat.

Ryder unfastened the man and lowered him to the floor carefully. He pressed hunting socks from a nearby display to either side of the blade, hoping to stanch the blood flow and knowing it wouldn't help. This man needed a surgeon, not a failing marshal. "Help is on the way," he assured the man, who was still reaching for a hold on Ryder's arms. "My brother's a medic and a deputy. He'll be here any second, and ambulances are on the way." Ryder sent texts to Cole and dispatch, his blood pressure rising with every keystroke.

The watchman continued to clutch at Ryder's sleeve and wave a trembling hand near his shoulder. Ryder followed the direction of his wild gaze to a stack of boxes behind him. Lighter fluid.

KARA STRAINED TO see what was happening. Ryder had called for the intruder to freeze. To put his hands up, then nothing more. For a few moments she could see both men, then they seemed to have disappeared. Had they run? Were they on the floor?

She inched through the shadows, too terrified to stay put, not knowing what might happen. What might have *already* happened. Her heart hammered with indecision. How far could she stray from where Ryder had left her? Where the hell was Cole?

The rough palm of one broad hand clamped over her mouth, and her frame went rigid.

A thick arm wrapped her in its iron grip, smashing her ribs. A hunting knife was clutched in her assailant's long fingers. "Your marshal has a bad habit of ruining things for me," he said, as the sounds of a police siren registered outside the door. "Now, come on. Before the cavalry arrives."

Kara didn't have to see his face. She knew that voice. The man from the park. Timothy Sand. She dug her feet into the concrete floor beneath her, hoping to stall him long enough for Cole to arrive or Ryder to come back for her, but Sand was too strong, and the tip of his blade dug precariously against her shirt.

"If you struggle, I will kill you," he promised, rancid breath streaming over her cheek. "Casey deserves better than to be an orphan, don't you think?"

The word struck ice through her veins. *Orphan.* For the first time since becoming Casey's mother, it was her own life that seemed unbearably fragile. She nodded slowly.

"Good." He edged her toward the elevator. One floor later, he guided her to the balcony, where a display of toboggans and mannequins in ski gear looked out over the floor below.

A pair of paramedics raced through the first-floor entrance, shuttling a gurney in the direction Ryder had disappeared. Cole followed on their heels.

A sudden blinding flood of fluorescent lighting

snapped on overhead, and Sand started. His left hand loosened over her mouth, and the knife in his right sliced swiftly through the thin material of her shirt and tender flesh below.

"Ahh," she cried, the pain searing through her.

"Freeze!" Ryder yelled from his position below. His seething voice boomed through the cavernous store. "You've got nowhere to go, Sand." He raised his gun. "Release her and step away now, and you might still get out of this alive."

Cole rushed to Ryder's side, matching his stance, gun drawn.

Behind them West ran toward the elevator.

Sand sighed into the hair at her ear. "I guess I have to go for now. Next time, you won't be this lucky." He released her without warning, his hands flowing instantly to her back. And he pushed.

Kara's feet fumbled, and her arms flailed as she was propelled off the display's end and into the open air. She screamed again as the floor came rushing toward her. Thoughts of her precious baby girl flickered in her mind.

Casey would be an orphan.

The sounds of gunfire burst around her; the fall seemed impossibly long. Her ears rang and her tummy lurched.

Ryder was in motion. Did he think he could catch her?

Their bodies collided as he dove at her, tackling into her before she met the unforgiving floor with a bone-jarring thud. Air rushed from her lungs as they tumbled over the camping display, through a tent and over bedrolls and sleeping bags before bursting apart.

Cole slid on his knees to their side. "Are you both okay? Is anything broken?" His eyes jumped from Kara's face to Ryder's. "That was insane!"

Ryder grunted, sucking in air. He forced himself onto his side with a wince. "Kara?"

"I'm okay," she sobbed, rolling to face him. Tears rolled hot and thick over her cheeks and his shirt. "Thank you."

Ryder enveloped her in his life-saving embrace. "I should never have brought you here."

THE GENTLE CLINKING of silverware and shifting of plates grew louder with each aching step toward the Garretts' bustling kitchen. Kara had had the worst night of her life, but it was time to put on a brave face for Casey, even if her ribs were bruised and so was most of the rest of her body. The cut on her side hadn't even required stitches, just some medical tape and a good cleaning.

However injured Ryder was, he didn't let on. At least nothing was broken.

Casey squealed in delight at the sight of her mama, and kicked her tiny feet beneath the high chair tray.

"Hello, gorgeous," Kara said, kissing her baby's head, cheeks and chubby, dimpled fists.

Mr. and Mrs. Garrett flanked the high chair at

a small dinette in the nook. "Good morning," they said in near unison.

Mrs. Garrett wiped a dollop of rice cereal from the high chair tray. "Help yourselves when you're ready."

A spread of breakfast foods lined the countertop.

Cole and West were seated at the island, dressed in matching khaki-and-brown uniforms, plates piled high from the extensive buffet.

Beyond the open back door, their oldest brother, Blake, paced with a cell phone pressed to his ear. His navy T-shirt and jeans seemed oddly casual for an FBI agent, but she supposed he wasn't really on duty, and a suit was overkill for any reason in Shadow Point. He lifted a hand in silent greeting when he saw her watching. Apparently, stopping Sand had become an official all-Garretts-on-deck situation.

Kara returned the wave, then busied herself freeing Casey from the high chair. She felt the weight of a dozen Garrett eyes on her as she wiped Casey's hands and face, trying not to get any breakfast on her pretty sundress or booties.

Ryder moseyed toward the coffeepot, fatigue in his eyes. "Any sightings since last night?"

West shook his head. "Nothing viable. The deputies have followed up on everything we had."

"At least everyone made it out alive," Mrs. Garrett said, her cheeks going pale with the words. "Tell me the security guard lived."

"He did," Cole answered, wiping his mouth on a

napkin. "Ryder saved his life. If he'd waited to get him down or put pressure on the wound, he wouldn't have made it to the hospital. The knife missed his carotid. He was damn lucky."

Ryder sipped his coffee. He didn't seem to think *lucky* was the right word. "We stopped Sand from making off with ten cases of lighter fluid. That's something."

The back door slapped shut as Blake walked inside. "Tech traced the photo from the printer to the drug store on Maple about forty minutes before they closed last night, which supports the theory he set the kindling and M-80s in place earlier. Then delivered the photo to move you to the station."

Kara cuddled Casey closer and moved toward the brothers. "So, he set it all up, knowing you'd take me there?"

West nodded. "I'm not surprised. Sand has been running from the law long enough to know how we operate."

Kara felt her mouth downturn. "Great."

"It's not a bad thing," West said. "Sand knows our protocols and he'll expect us to follow them."

"And you're going to change things up?" she guessed.

Cole frowned. "No. We're going to do exactly what he expects us to do so he thinks he has the upper hand, and when he shows up feeling overly confident, we'll be waiting to arrest him."

Kara cast her gaze around the room, suddenly uncomfortable. "When he shows up where? Here?"

"No." Ryder returned to her side with a plate of food, concern lining his brow. "Right now, Sand doesn't know where you are, but he'll be looking. That means we have the upper hand. There's a deputy stationed outside your house and tech added surveillance cameras to the utility poles near the sheriff's department in case he goes there looking."

Blake swiveled his cell phone to face her. A black-and-white image of a car from the alley outside the camping store centered the screen. "Footage collected from the drug store confirmed that he's driving the older-model white sedan you saw last night. We're circling the wagons, and it'll squeeze him out."

Kara didn't share Blake's confidence or enthusiasm about their progress so far. Maybe he'd feel differently if Sand had thrown him off a second-story balcony. "Why didn't the car come up as stolen when Ryder called in the plates?"

"The owner is on vacation," West answered. "When I spoke to him, he was shocked to hear it wasn't in his garage."

Ryder rubbed her back. "Every criminal makes a mistake eventually, and Sand's mistake was coming here."

The Garretts lifted their coffee mugs in unison. A toast to Ryder's words.

Kara leaned against his side, hoping to absorb even the smallest measure of his confidence, but the moment was cut short by the sounds of multiple dings and buzzes.

The Garrett brothers lifted their cell phones and swiped the screens.

"Turn on the news," Ryder called.

Cole flashed to the little television lodged in the corner of the kitchen.

Mrs. Garrett went for the larger flat screen in the family room. "Which channel?"

"Any," Ryder said through gritted teeth.

Both televisions settled on the same distant image of a burning cornfield. Different news anchors reported from the foreground. A woman cornered the little screen in the kitchen. A balding man in glasses was on the television in the family room. Behind them blazed a ring of fire twenty feet across and nearly as high.

A trio of scarecrows were arranged in the center.

Kara covered her mouth as the helicopter covering the scene on the kitchen television circled lower, making the figures more visible. A large cardboard star had been cut out and staked through the first scarecrow's chest. *US MARSHAL* was scratched across it in thick, heavy lines.

Two other scarecrows lay on the ground at the base of the first's support post.

"That guy's you," Cole said to Ryder, "but what's that supposed to mean?" He marched up to the television and pointed at the other two prone figures.

West joined Cole a foot from the screen, hip

cocked, both hands gripping his waist. "Is that us on the ground?"

Cole hacked a deep, throaty noise. "Think again, Sand."

Blake swore under his breath and shot Ryder a pointed look. Ryder nodded, short and quick.

Kara watched Ryder for an explanation. He and Blake had seen something there the other brothers hadn't.

Mr. Garrett set his steaming coffee mug aside and crossed the room to the television. He studied the scene with clear, discerning eyes. "Must've taken some time to do this. It's precise." He waved his pointer finger in a circle, indicating the line of fire. "He had to have wet down the field to stop the flames from spreading in this weather. A drought, really. We haven't had a lick of rain in more than a month. I sure hope Farmer Mays has good insurance. That's going to ruin his crop."

Kara turned back to the image, mesmerized. "Is this meant for us?" she asked the room. Her heart hammered and her tummy ached. "Is this his big move?"

Ryder gave a stiff dip of his chin. "It's a threat."

"Was anyone hurt?"

"No. He wants us to react."

Kara breathed easier, knowing no one had been hurt in Sand's attempt to get to them. "He wants you to go to the scene?" she guessed. "All of you, or just you?" she asked Ryder.

He locked eyes with her then. "He wants me out of hiding. I suppose if your entire detail went to the scene and left you alone, he wouldn't complain, either." Ryder turned to his parents. "We won't spend another night here, and you should consider visiting Aunt Linda in Lexington. It won't take him long to get your address from someone in town."

His mom barked a laugh. His dad ignored him completely.

Kara imagined the Garretts would rather go down fighting. Their sons had gotten the disposition honestly.

Before she could beg Mr. and Mrs. Garrett to reconsider, something small and yellow caught her eye in the blazing cornfield. "Oh, no. Look." She gripped Ryder's arm with one hand and tucked Casey more tightly against her with the other. The little yellow figure came more clearly into view as the helicopter swooped in. "It's Rosie," she whispered.

Ryder turned angry eyes on Kara. "The doll?" His gaze slid to Casey, then to his brothers.

"Who?" Cole asked.

"She was mine when I was young," Kara said. "I gave her to Casey when she was born, and I forgot her at my house when we left yesterday."

Recollection was written on West's face.

Ryder swore.

Kara let her desperate gaze drift from face-to-face

through the room. "That doll in the yellow raincoat belongs to Casey. The figures on the ground aren't other lawmen. They're me and my daughter."

Chapter Ten

Ryder turned his back to the television as his brothers broke into action, scraping plates into the sink and pressing cell phones to their ears. Pain and regret tugged Ryder's heart as he pulled Kara and Casey against him. He'd known Sand wouldn't stay quiet for long, but he'd hoped they could at least finish breakfast before all hell broke loose.

Kara wound her arms around his middle and rested her cheek against his chest. Her heart pounded furiously against him and there was a distinct shudder to her breaths.

"This will be okay," he promised, lowering his lips to her ear. "No one was hurt. That field is on the other side of town. We're safe here, and we have time to plot out the best course of action."

She rocked her head back, bringing her chin to rest where her cheek had been. She rolled frightened blue eyes up at him. Her fingers curled into the fabric of his shirt.

"I mean it," he said. "And you should eat. It's looking like a busy day."

Kara gave a soft groan, then pulled away.

Casey tried to take Ryder's shirt with her, her tiny fingers tugging the fabric of his sleeve. Her little arm outstretched as Kara shifted away, but didn't offer release.

Ryder reached for her then. "How about I hold her while you eat?" he asked Kara.

Burning cornfields and making scarecrows into bizarre voodoo dolls were behaviors way outside Sand's norm, and Ryder had no idea what would come next. Kara needed to eat and rest now because here, in the safety and shelter of his family home, surrounded by lawmen, retired and otherwise, she was still safe. This was the time to fill her belly and prepare for whatever awaited them.

She turned Casey over to Ryder with a quick kiss, then wrapped her arms around her middle. "I don't think I can eat," she said, "but I should probably get dressed."

He cuddled Casey into his arms and kissed Kara's forehead. "We can take some fruit and muffins with us. In case you get hungry later." Or they were forced into hiding somewhere they wouldn't have easy access to anything worth digesting.

Casey released his shirtsleeve in favor of gnawing her fist.

Kara marched woodenly up the staircase, eyes glued on Casey until she disappeared onto the next floor.

The kitchen stilled in her absence.

His brothers stared, no longer rapt in their phones.

"What?"

Silence.

Casey pulled her tiny hand from her mouth and slapped it against Ryder's cheek. A string of slobber stretched between them.

"Nothing," West said flatly. "Just looking. That's all."

Cole chuckled. "You just got slapped by a baby."

Blake only shook his head and went back to tapping hard on his phone screen.

Ryder's phone buzzed, and he struggled to free it from his pocket.

"Here." His mom came to take Casey.

If Ryder wanted any time to get to know Kara's baby, he'd have to carve it out when his mom wasn't around.

"I have an idea," his mom said, gathering the infant into her arms. "What if I take Casey and Kara to Aunt Susie's farm across the river while you boys handle things here?"

"I don't know," Ryder said, immediately missing the weight and warmth of Casey in his arms. "That's a big property. We don't have enough manpower to guard it and look for Sand at the same time."

"No," Blake said, butting into the conversation. "Mom's idea is a good one. It's smart to go to Susie's. Sand wouldn't know to look for her there. Susie isn't even our real aunt. There's no logical link for him to follow. Dad can go with them and keep a tight perimeter around the house only. Mom can keep Kara and Casey inside."

Their mom dropped a floppy sunhat on Casey's head. "She has her own disguise." She tugged the brim low on the baby's head. "No one will recognize her now." She beamed into the baby's face. "Look at this angel. The hat matches her booties. I'm fit to die."

"Well, don't do that," Cole said, "you're on baby-sitting duty."

West stuffed his brown sheriff's hat onto his big head and went for the back door. "My guy at Kara's house said there was no movement all night, so Sand must've been there and taken the doll before my deputy arrived."

That left a narrow window. Ryder wondered idly if Sand might've been at Kara's yesterday while he and West had searched the ground outside for footprints.

He pinched the bridge of his nose and tried to stay focused. All the bad that had come from Ryder's last run-in with Sand didn't compare to the amount of potential damage that could be done now. He'd barely gotten Kara back, *if* he'd gotten her back. They hadn't talked about reuniting officially. She'd just said that she still loved him, and he'd reciprocated. There had been a kiss after that, but Ryder had no doubt that Kara would walk away in a heartbeat if she thought he wasn't good for Casey.

Ryder knew he would be. He'd be everything he could for both of them.

He watched his mother sing softly to Kara's daughter. His mom looked truly happy, but Casey looked so fragile.

Could he protect Kara *and* Casey? Could he capture Sand before he hurt someone else this time? He drifted closer to his mother and the sweet baby girl in her arms. "We'll get him," he told his mother, setting a hand on her back.

"I know."

The sound of Kara's footfalls came from the steps, and Ryder turned to see her.

She'd traded the pajamas for a pair of cutoff shorts, a faded red T-shirt and running shoes. "Ready," she said, a look of determination on her brow.

He tried not to imagine running the palms of his hands up her long tan legs and turning those shorts inside out.

"I want to go to my house," she said. "Sand took Rainy Rosie off the couch, so I know he was inside. I want to salvage whatever I can before he burns the place down. Assuming that was what the fire in the cornfield meant." She had a brave face in place. "I'm okay with Casey going away for the day. I heard you talking while I changed."

Ryder frowned. "You heard that? And you don't mind parting from her?"

She gave a sad smile. "Old house. Thin walls. Honestly, I'd prefer Casey wasn't with us while we run home. It's probably best if Casey lay low." Her voice cracked on the final sentence, her bravado a nearly convincing facade. "If Sand is watching, he'll assume Casey's with me. With us. She'll be safer with your folks, and I can't live knowing I've put her in any more danger today."

"Okay," Ryder said. "I'll take you home to get whatever you want. Mom and Dad will take Casey to Aunt Susie's for the day." He scanned the room for anyone in disagreement.

Kara walked to his mom's side and took Casey into her arms. "I love you," she whispered. "I'll see you soon, so be good for Mrs. Garrett and try not to worry. Ryder and his family are going to protect us."

Ryder struggled to swallow the brick of emotion growing larger in his throat. Whatever happened, he couldn't let Casey or Kara get hurt. His heart had become irrevocably tied to them. He'd never stopped loving Kara, so it made sense that he'd fallen so easily into his old thought patterns and instincts with her, but Casey was new, and his desire to guard and protect her was something completely *other*. Nothing so sweet and fragile should have ever come to be in Sand's path.

His brothers moved in on him then, phones in hand, delivering reports and updates from their contacts in the field.

"No activity," West reported. "It's quiet at Kara's and at the station. I've got two plain-clothed deputies at the fire, too. So far, no signs of Sand."

Blake hooked an elbow on the island behind him. "That's smart. Arsonists are known for watching their fires burn. We might still find him there, enjoying the spectacle."

Ryder agreed. "Okay. Good. Meanwhile, Kara and I will go to her place. Get what she needs and get out. We'll meet Mom, Dad and Casey at Aunt Susie's afterward."

Kara swayed slowly to his side, a sleeping baby in her arms. Casey's little head rested on her mama's chest, rising and falling with Kara's every breath.

Ryder's mom hooked a giant purse over her shoulder and palmed the keys to his SUV. The sadness in her eyes was enough to break his heart. "Take your father's truck instead. Leave your SUV in the barn for now. Sand will be looking for that. We'll take my Ford to Susie's."

Reluctantly, Kara shifted her baby into Mrs. Garrett's arms. "Protect her," she whispered.

His mom's eyes glossed with emotion he'd never seen before. "With my life," she pledged.

The ride to Kara's home from the Garretts' homestead had never seemed longer. To make matters worse, Kara's mind was split with worry for Casey and fear for the town. She sent up continual prayers for her daughter's safe passage to the farm across the river, adding a round of pleas for herself and Ryder in between.

Kara wanted Casey to grow up with a loving

mother at her side, not a horror story about a monster who came to town and killed her. She wanted to grow old watching Casey grow up, maybe even Casey's children, too. Kara wanted to watch them change the world, and if she was really lucky, she hoped Ryder would want to do that with her.

The truck came to a stop in her driveway, and Ryder climbed out with one hand on his weapon. "Two minutes," he said before closing his door and locking her inside the vehicle. He walked the length of her house, then vanished around the back.

Kara checked the clock on the dash, then scanned the scene beyond her window. Two minutes later, Ryder reappeared with a stiff nod.

She jumped out, too anxious to sit still any longer. "All clear?"

"Outside, yeah," he said with a flick of his gaze to the small black Mustang across the street. "West's deputy's here. He'll keep watch from the front. Once we go inside, you need to wait in the foyer, door locked behind you, while I check the house."

Kara nodded.

She followed his instructions inside, until he returned to her once more, this time looking somewhat at ease. "All clear. Where was Rosie when you left yesterday?"

"On the couch."

Kara hefted a plastic tote from her hall closet and dumped the contents onto the floor. If she was lucky, those things would still be there when she came back, *not burned*. And hopefully that would be soon.

If Sand burned her house down, it wouldn't matter about the mess.

"I'm going to put a few things in here to store at your folks' house, if that's okay. Nothing I need. Stuff I don't want to lose. Just in case."

Ryder's solemn expression made it clear that he understood and, apparently, he agreed that losing her house in this mess was a possibility.

She turned away then, leaving Ryder to peer through the front windows while she collected a second round of favorite things from her home. She started with the framed photos from the fireplace mantel. "Where do you think he is?" Did he really think there was a chance Sand was outside now? Wouldn't the deputy stationed out front have seen him? Her mouth dried further. He'd walked right up to the back door while deputies sat out front before.

"I don't know." Ryder dropped the edge of her curtain and stepped back from the window facing the small side yard. "I hate that he's out there plotting his next move, and I'm playing defense. I should be chasing him and not the other way around."

Kara set the plastic tote on the couch. Déjà vu pricked and snapped against her skin. It wasn't the first time she'd stood helplessly by while Ryder longed to be somewhere else—*chasing Timothy Sand*, specifically—but it felt just as abysmal. She told herself not to feel betrayed. They'd shared a kiss last night. Nothing more. Emotions had been running high, and chemistry had never been one of their problems. He certainly didn't owe her a happily-ever-after because of it.

Ryder released a long, labored breath and turned arresting blue eyes on her. "I'd thought chasing Sand was long behind me."

Kara moved into him, letting Ryder's strong arms form a protective cocoon around her.

"Then again," he said, "I'd thought a lot of things were behind me."

Kara fought to keep the emotion away from her expression as the same old worry came to mind. Could Ryder really put her and Casey first, whatever might come?

"How are you holding up?" he asked.

"Not well," she admitted, refocusing on the bigger issue. "I feel like we're playing Sand's game without knowing any of the rules."

"Doesn't matter what his rules are. He's in our town now, and he's going to wish he hadn't come here."

Kara hoped he was right. "What do you think the fire in the field meant?" The answer seemed obvious. Sand planned to burn them or maybe just burn the world down around them, but Ryder had studied Sand for years, and she suspected he saw something more this morning when the fire flared through the television screens.

Ryder watched her for a long beat before speak-

ing. "I think it was retaliation. He didn't like having his face plastered all over the news yesterday,
so he returned the gesture with me in the form of a
scarecrow. I put his image out there to let everyone
know I'm after him."

"And he did the same." Kara's pulse quickened.
"You think he was publicly announcing his intentions like you did."

"I do." Ryder's voice was low then, fierce. "I won't
let him take you and Casey from me." His warm
breath tickled her face as he planted kisses along her
forehead, cheeks and chin. His sweet words melted
her heart and loosened her knees until she was sure
she couldn't stay upright without his help.

Slowly, Ryder pressed his mouth to hers, kissing
her fully and deeply until the world fell away. His
lips made promises she knew he couldn't keep. Not
while they were being hunted. But hopefully he'd
make good on them very soon.

She stepped back in a daze, enjoying the flood of
desire rolling through her core. "I should get busy."

He loosened his grip, but didn't let go. His heated
gaze raked over her body, obviously thinking the same
thing she had been. There was a bedroom just up the
steps. A couch behind them. Floor all around. Kara
knew firsthand about the toe-curling, earth-stopping
pleasures that came after a look like that, and she was
tempted to ask for them.

Until the blazing cornfield crept back into her
mind, and a chill slid down her spine.

Kara stumbled back to collect herself, then lifted her tote and moved to the next room in search of irreplaceable items. "I'll hurry," she called over her shoulder.

In the kitchen, she braced the bag against one hip and plucked the fabric of her shirt away from her chest, trying to settle down. It was time to be real. Last night's confession of love didn't come with promises. Just kisses. He could easily go straight back to Ohio when this was over and leave her heartbroken. The only thing she could afford to think about right now was Casey.

Head in the game, Kara treated the house like a grid and worked methodically from room to room, tossing treasured books, photo albums and keepsakes into the tote for their salvation. When she reached her bedroom, she made a direct path to the bedside drawer.

Her feet slowed as the nightstand came into view. The top drawer, where she kept her most private memories, was pulled slightly open. "Ryder?" she called.

Had he and West searched the house when they came by yesterday? He'd told her there was no new evidence of Sand's visit outside the home, but had he and West been in her room? Had they seen the drawer full of Ryder's old love letters and the stacks of accompanying photos? He hadn't said so, but maybe he thought it would embarrass her. It might have at the time, but after her confession on the porch swing, the collection would've made more sense. She'd never had the heart to let anything of his go.

Regardless. The drawer had been shut when she last stood in her bedroom.

"Yeah?" Ryder's voice echoed up the stairwell, accompanied by quick-falling footsteps.

Kara moved closer, curling her fingers around the drawer's handle. "When you and West were here yesterday," she began, tugging the drawer wide before Ryder made it into the room. "Did you—" Her gaze landed on the blackened contents and her heart jerked into a sprint. She stumbled back on a sharp intake of air, bumping her legs against the bed.

"What?" He strode through the open doorway.

Kara jumped.

"What's wrong?"

She turned her eyes to the nightstand. A partially burned book of matches lay inside the drawer atop the love letters, engagement photos and a million other things Kara had clung to in Ryder's absence. Someone had painstakingly scorched the edges of everything. Melting and curling the photos' corners, singeing and charring the paper, without letting any of it be completely destroyed.

Ryder swore. He dragged his phone from his pocket and pressed it to his ear.

Kara scooted onto her bed, pressing her back against the headboard and clutching her knees to her chest. Somewhere in the back of her mind, she'd created a false image of Sand rushing into and out of her home, grabbing Rainy Rosie, the first thing he saw. Her gaze returned to the letters and she held herself more tightly. This was…meticulous. He'd taken his time. What else had he touched? Infected? How long had he spent invading the privacy of her life? Her stomach knotted impossibly tighter.

Ryder's voice carried on beside her, conveying the findings to West, then speaking with what she assumed was another marshal.

The landline rang beside her, and her hand shot out to answer on instinct. "Hello." Her voice quavered, still unsteady from the shock of the ruined keepsakes.

"Mrs. Garrett?" a familiar voice asked. The voice, she realized with a drop of her stomach, was the one from the park and the camping store. "No, no, no," he corrected himself. "Sorry about that. I've learned I was wrong. It seems you are the *almost*-Mrs. Garrett."

Kara made a strangled sound, suddenly unable to breathe.

"Kara?" Ryder dove onto the bed beside her, dropping his cell phone on the pillow. He mouthed, "Is this him?"

Kara wobbled her head, still straining for air as fear clutched her windpipe.

Ryder took the receiver from her shaking hand and held it on his open palm, pressing the speaker option with his fingertip.

"Speechless?" Sand taunted. "I've had that effect

on a number of people." He chuckled darkly. "I've lost track of how many. But I didn't call to talk about me. I wanted to talk about you, and that little princess of yours. She looks so lovely today, doesn't she? In her little sundress with the matching booties and bonnet." He clucked his tongue. "It's good that you dressed her for the weather. I'm afraid it's going to be a scorcher."

The sound of a striking match sizzled through the line, and Kara's body jolted forward, heart seizing.

"No!" she screamed. Her breath coming back to her in a powerful rush. "Don't hurt my baby," she cried.

Ryder jerked the phone from her hand. "Sand!"

"Don't touch her," Kara grappled Ryder's shoulder, lunging closer to the receiver, ready to pledge her soul in exchange for Casey's safety.

But it was too late. The line was already dead.

Chapter Eleven

Kara launched from the bed, her limbs weak and clumsy with shock. "We have to go." She swung her arm out for Ryder, but her hand collided with the tote she'd so carefully packed instead. Keepsakes and treasured memories scattered across her bedroom floor with a crash. "Oh!" she squeaked, jumping wide and tangling her feet in an attempt not to step on the beloved contents.

Ryder's long arm snaked out to catch her as her knees weakened. His lean frame was beside her in seconds, pulling her against him. "Stop." His voice was low and even, but his grip was firm.

She stood, shell-shocked, as a fist of emotion punched through her chest, and the world tilted. "Come on. Hurry!" Kara tried to take another step forward, but Ryder wouldn't be moved.

His sinewy arms tightened around her middle. "Kara," he said coolly. "Wait."

"Wait for what?" she snapped, jerking herself free. "For him to kill her?" Bile flooded her tongue, rejecting the words. A bead of sweat broke on her forehead.

"No." Ryder shook his head slowly, purposefully. "But we can't just run off and lead him straight to her."

Kara considered the notion. "He's already there," she croaked through a constricting throat. "He saw her hat and booties."

"We don't know that," Ryder said, "and we can't take a liar's word."

Kara worked to relax her stance. "Then, what?"

"Well, first, we can't get overemotional and react to his stimuli. That's how he wins. He sets up the scene he wants to unfold, then waits while we rush in and act it out for him, and we can't afford to do that."

Kara's limbs had stilled, bur her heart and lungs worked double-time beneath her rib cage, pinching and aching with each wild thump. "I think he's got her. Ryder. He's got my baby girl."

"My parents would have called."

"What if they *can't*." Horror and nausea pulled at her core. "I sent Casey away to keep her safe, and now she's the one in danger." The words were whispers, barely audible against the ringing in her ears. "He knew what Casey was wearing."

He struck a match.

Kara clamped a hand over her mouth. "I'm going to be sick." She raced to the adjoining bathroom and retched until it hurt to breathe.

Ryder lowered to his knees beside her. He pulled

her hair away from her face and offered a wet wash-cloth for her thrumming head. "I've already spoken with West. I was on the phone with him when I heard Sand on your line. He had just checked on Casey. Mom and Aunt Susie are playing peek-a-boo with her in the den. It's in the center of the house with multiple exit options from that point. Dad's got it covered. Casey's okay." He cupped her face in his confident hands, bringing their gazes to meet. "There's no one at Susie's farm who shouldn't be, and West is on his way for added cover. Just in case."

Kara wanted his words to be true, but what if he was wrong? "He has to be near. He saw her."

Ryder nodded. "I think it's most likely that he was watching my folks' home and saw her there before we all left. My parents' place is well fortified and monitored by a security company, but it's also the obvious place for us to have hidden. It wouldn't have taken Sand long to find us there."

"What if he followed them?" she asked, her voice shaky, her tummy sick. "What if he's lying in wait at Susie's? Maybe your dad just hasn't seen him yet."

"I don't think so." He hooked a swath of hair behind her ear and leveled her with calm, confident eyes. "When we split up with my folks, Sand could only go one way. We know he chose to follow us because he called us here. He couldn't have known we'd come here unless he'd followed."

Kara slumped into a seated position, leaning

against her bathtub for support. "So, he didn't follow your parents? He doesn't know where they are?"

"I don't think so, no."

She pressed the washcloth to her eyes. "And, he's here somewhere?" Her stomach churned painfully once more. "Watching us?"

Ryder didn't answer. He didn't have to. He'd already said as much, and the look on his face said so much more. The set of his jaw and color of his skin. The fists clenched tightly against the bathroom floor.

Kara released a long breath and set the washcloth aside. Sand wasn't with her daughter.

Casey was safe.

"Feeling better?"

"Yeah." Kara pulled herself up by the sink and rinsed her mouth out. If Casey was okay, then she would be, too. "What do we do next?"

Ryder strode back to the bedroom and refilled the toppled tote. "We collect your things as planned and take them away from here."

Kara moved to the nightstand and stared at her ruined letters. "I can't take them. Can I?"

"Not those," he said. "Those are evidence now."

Her bottom lip trembled, but she nodded in heartbreaking acceptance. Her lovely treasures would soon be read by tech support, by strangers and by his brothers. She turned her eyes to Ryder.

"I'll write you more letters." He looped a strong arm around her shoulder and pulled her near. "You don't want those memories anymore. When we're finished with Sand, I'm making it my mission to eradicate everything he's tainted. He can have the letters. Those are pieces of the past. We'll make better memories in the future."

Her heart swelled with hope and regret. The ever-present tornado of emotion continued to churn and twist inside her. "People are going to read those," she said.

Ryder gave a sad smile. "I know. It doesn't matter. Everything in those letters was true. Is true," he corrected. "And anyone who can't relate to those kinds of feelings, the love, the desire—" he rested his forehead on hers "—those people should be damn jealous." He kissed her head and hefted the refilled tote into the sharp V of his side, securing it with his free arm. "Right now, we should go. I'll look out for Sand, and we'll sneak over the river to Aunt Susie's so you can see Casey's okay."

Kara squeezed him tight before setting him free. "Thank you." She looked beyond him to the silence outside her room. "Maybe you should lead the way."

Ryder passed her the tote and removed his sidearm before descending the stairs.

The house was still. No signs of an unwelcome guest.

Ryder repeated his perimeter sweeps inside and out before escorting Kara to the truck.

He folded himself behind the wheel and connected his phone to the truck's Bluetooth. "Call Mom."

"Calling Mom," the truck answered as he reversed onto the road. Hearing that Casey was safe, directly from his mother, would put Kara's mind at ease, and she desperately needed that.

Kara's skin was pale and her gaze was jumpy, as she searched endlessly outside the window. Her knee bobbed and her fingers worked a thread from her shirt until he thought the entire garment would unravel.

Ryder locked stares with the undercover deputy in the black Mustang, dipping his chin only slightly in acknowledgment, unwilling to give the man away if Sand was watching. West would fill him in on what they'd found in Kara's room. Ryder needed to get Kara out of there and check on Casey.

He turned back to the road with a grimace. He and West had been on Kara's property after the fire at the sheriff's department, looking for booby traps and trace evidence of Sand's presence, and they'd left before the lookout had arrived. Their haste had given Sand time to sneak inside, steal the doll and ruin Kara's letters.

The ringing stopped and the call went to voice mail.

Kara's muscles stiffened visibly. Her cheeks flushed, and she cracked the window, sucking in deep breaths of free-flowing air.

Ryder redialed his mother several times before changing tactics. "Call Dad." Surely his father would answer. Ryder knew they were okay, logically, but the fact that his mother hadn't jumped on her phone was a point of concern. Hearing his dad clear things up would put his mind at ease and help Kara to relax on the long drive to Aunt Susie's across the river.

"Calling Dad," the truck agreed.

The call went to voice mail.

Kara jerked her face in his direction. "Call Susie," she told him. Desperation dripped from her words. "Maybe cell service is bad there. Try her landline."

Ryder grimaced. "I don't know Aunt Susie's number."

"What?" Tears welled in her wide blue eyes. "Then call West again," she demanded. "Call West."

"I just called West."

"Calling West," the truck agreed.

Ryder stifled a groan and checked the rearview one more time for a tail, then took the final turn out of Kara's neighborhood, through the main entrance that dipped dramatically through a historic brick-lined tunnel.

His truck hugged the hilly residential road, ducking quickly under the old railroad tracks by way of an arched cutout in the grassy hillside. The stubby passage was lined in elaborate landscaping and flagged with hand-carved signs announcing guests' arrival to Deer Hollow, a quaint, family-centric allotment perfect for raising children. None of the other neighborhoods they'd looked at three years ago had come close to appealing to the family man in him like this one had, and he'd been elated to know Kara loved it, too. She especially loved the entrance tunnel and sidewalks throughout the area.

Ryder breathed easier the moment his truck emerged from the tunnel without encountering any sort of ambush that Sand might have considered setting within. Still, Ryder couldn't shake the feeling Sand had called to rush them outside for something. So, what was it? Why had he called? Not just to scare them. That wasn't a big enough goal for someone like him.

Ryder checked his rearview once more. This time, an object appeared in the air, and Ryder slowed the truck to a stop, craning for a look at what was heading his way.

"What's wrong?" Kara asked. "Why are we stopping?"

"Garrett," West finally answered the call as the thing landed in the bed of his borrowed truck with a loud crash and an explosion of flames.

Kara screamed, twisting in her seat and staring wide-eyed through the rear window. Her chest rose and fell in sprinting puffs, and Ryder felt the familiar coil of rage rise up inside him.

FIRE WHOOSHED INTO the air, licking the glass between the cab and the bed. Smoke roiled into the air, obscuring the world around them.

He jammed the truck into Park and jumped onto the street, muscles tensed to spring. Adrenaline charged through his limbs as he surveilled the scene, staring into the veil of dark smoke. His fingers locked instinctually over the butt of his sidearm, waiting to spot his target.

"Out!" Ryder hollered, stealing a look at Kara, who was still frozen with fear inside the cab.

The flames in the truck bed burned low and dirty. A distraction. From what? He couldn't begin to guess, but it would be bad, and he needed backup.

Kara leapt from her seat, stumbling against her open door and asking a thousand questions he couldn't answer. *What was that? Where did it come from? What do we do? Is it Sand? Where is he?*

Ryder yanked opened the crew cab door, then unhinged the fire extinguisher he'd tossed inside before leaving his family farm. A must-have, he'd thought, for hunting an arsonist.

"Ryder?" West barked through the truck's speaker. "Where are you?"

"Outside Kara's neighborhood." He pulled the trigger on the extinguisher and aimed at the dancing flames.

A white chemical cloud lifted into the air, mingling with smoke from the suffocated flames.

Ryder scanned the scene in search of the only person who would do something like this.

Kara coughed her way to his side. "Are you okay?"

Another thump! Another round of broken glass and a fresh blast of flames.

"Dammit!" Ryder snuffed the fire and turned to the truck. "West! We're on Oakvale. He's tossing bottle bombs, and I can't see anything but this damn smoke."

"Already on the way," his brother answered.

A third bottle exploded into flames in the truck's bed. The hovering fog of chemicals from the extinguisher and smoke from the pint-size Molotov cocktails stung his nose and eyes.

Kara screamed and clutched him tighter.

Ryder's fury heated to a boil. "Sand!" he yelled into the smoke-filled air, his voice wild with rage. "Come out, you cowardly sonofabitch!"

Beyond the smoke and flame, a figure stood on the railroad tracks over the tunnel, another flaming bottle in one hand.

Kara gripped Ryder's elbow. "Sand."

"Change of plans," Ryder muttered. He handed the extinguisher to Kara and pulled his gun. "Pull this trigger, and keep your eyes on him. If he disappears get in the truck and lock the doors. Otherwise, keep the chemicals coming." He wiggled the extinguisher.

She nodded, unsure. "I'll try."

That was all he needed. Ryder turned with purpose toward the hill to the railroad tracks and bolted forward.

West's voice continued to make demands through his truck speakers. "Where are you? What is going on?"

Ryder crouched as he jogged, using the thinning smoke as cover for his approach, hoping to maintain the element of surprise as long as possible. The acrid air stung his lungs as he climbed the hill behind the Deer Hollow sign.

Another bottle hit Ryder's truck with the same crash and whoosh as the others. Kara kept the dry chemical cure going, rejuvenating the white cloud around her until she became nearly invisible behind it.

Ryder's feet slid on loose pebbles in the dried grass as he reached the abandoned tracks. The area was foggy, drenched in the pollution of too many homemade bombs and the effects of an active extinguisher. The ground was littered with ripped clothes and empty bottles. No Timothy Sand.

He'd lured Ryder there. The phone call had been meant to push him out of the neighborhood and through the tunnel. For what? To toss mini bottle bombs at his truck? To infuriate him and scare the daylights out of Kara? Was this just a game of cat and mouse now? An itch at the back of his mind turned his face toward the white cloud behind him. Could Sand have gotten to Kara while Ryder had been coming for him? Was that what this was for? Had Ryder done exactly what Sand wanted, all the while trying not to?

Ryder braced his arms, gun extended into the haze. He stepped carefully, putting the full extent of his training to work. His senses were on high alert. Muscles tensed to spring. Turning back for Kara might be exactly what Sand wanted him to do.

Ryder's thoughts circled uselessly, trying to guess the intentions of a madman.

The sickening sound of a lighting match struck at Ryder's heart, and he spun in search of the source.

Back on the road, the telltale slam of his truck door said that Kara had gotten inside.

That meant she was safe.

It also meant that Sand must have vanished from her view.

The chemicals thinned, revealing the taillights on his dad's truck as it rolled forward, away from the scene of the ambush.

Good girl, he thought. *Lead him away. Make him think I'm with you.*

"You're fast," a familiar voice taunted.

Sand's form took shape as the remnants of smoke drifted away. He had another burning bottle in his hand.

"Drop it, Sand."

"Gladly." He launched the bottle at Ryder's head.

The flame scorched his hand and face as he attempted to deflect the crudely made bomb. The bottle landed and bounced on the ground without breaking, but the fire raced to consume the spilled fuel.

Skin burning and temper flaring, Ryder was forced to stop and stomp the flames along the old railroad track, kicking mounds of gravel and dirt onto the fire until it was satisfactorily snuffed out. To let it burn would have been to ignite the town in this seemingly endless drought.

Ryder whipped his head up then, spinning in a tight circle to hunt Sand, who was already down the hill and fleeing at full speed toward a small red sedan.

"Stop!" Ryder gave chase, easily closing the distance Sand had created. He'd gotten older and heavier while Ryder had gotten fitter and more fine-tuned.

The blessed sounds of emergency vehicle sirens cried in the distance.

West was on the way. Along with a fire truck and possibly an ambulance. Another good thing. The firemen would need to deal with the abandoned bomb-making materials on the railroad tracks.

Ryder's feet hit the street as Sand reached the car. "Freeze, Sand!" Ryder hollered. He braced his arms and leveled his Glock in line with Sand's back. A torso shot would bring him down so that Ryder could bring him in.

The growling of a massive engine drew Ryder's eyes to the road behind them. His dad's truck raced forward, practically out of control and seemingly straight for Timothy Sand. Kara's determined face was at work behind the wheel. Ryder jumped back. She looked as crazy as any mother whose infant's life had been threatened one too many times in a day, and for a moment he wondered if she planned to run Sand down.

Sand turned and ran. He passed the sedan and slowed, looking angrily over his shoulder. If that wasn't his ride, then where was he going? Surely he didn't expect to beat Ryder at a footrace.

Ryder dashed forward. "Hands where I can see

them," he demanded, a sense of cautious victory playing in his chest. He hoped Kara would slow when she saw Ryder had Sand cornered, but the engine only growled louder.

The big black truck tore a path between him and the arsonist with a screech of burning rubber, instantly blocking his view of Sand. Kara slammed the beast to a hard, rocking stop, already screaming, "Get in!" Her voice burst through the open windows.

She didn't have to ask twice. Something was undeniably wrong. It was written in the terror on her face. Whatever she needed Ryder for, she'd decided it was more important than capturing Sand, and that made the matter unimaginable.

Ryder bounced onto the bench seat, eyes fixed on the fleeing lunatic visible outside the windshield. "Chase him," he said. "Don't hit him, but don't let him get away!"

Before he could close the door behind him, the red sedan exploded in a teeth-rattling eruption. The truck rocked under the force. Ryder's ears rang and his vision blurred. The car he'd expected Sand to get into and race away in had blown three feet off the ground before plummeting back to earth in a flaming disaster. A wave of heat rushed out to meet them like an angry apparition, sweeping over the windshield and hovering above the ground outside.

Kara panted behind the wheel, then shifted into Reverse and tore away from the scene, separating Ryder from Sand yet again.

She shifted roughly into Park at a safer distance and sobbed outright. "West told me," she cried. "Sand bought explosives from a demolition website last week. The team tracing his financials found a record of the purchase today. They're looking at everything he's been doing since his probation ended, trying to guess his plan, and they found that. West said to be careful, but you were already alone with him, and I just…" She set her forehead on the steering wheel and cried.

Ryder sorted the words, thankful the team was making progress in tracing Sand's recent activity and especially glad that those strides had saved his life. *Kara* had saved his life.

A funny thing occurred to him then. "You weren't going to run him over?"

She rocked her forehead against the wheel until her puffy eyes came into view. "No," she half laughed, half scoffed. "I was coming for you. I thought I was too late."

Ryder turned to stare at the flaming car. The place Sand had last been seen. "I thought I had him."

Before he'd disappeared into the smoke and vanished.

Chapter Twelve

Emergency vehicles flooded the scene, dividing and conquering. Crime scene crews gingerly packed the bottle-bomb materials found on the train tracks. Deputies fanned out across the area searching for clues and examining the path Sand had taken to the exploding car. Firemen contained the fire, soaking the grass with water and applying a thick layer of chemicals to stanch the beating flames. Marshals tracked Sand's escape route through Kara's neighborhood, but he was long gone.

Ryder was the first marshal to give up. He dragged himself back into the chaos, past the charred sedan, past the place where he'd almost become a pile of ashes, back to Kara.

He'd gone after the arsonist once the car had finished exploding and settled into low flames, but Sand's trail had gone cold. The other marshals arrived later and stayed behind to canvass for sightings. Ryder needed to get back to Kara.

Kara stood in a tight triangle with Cole and Uncle

Henry outside the doors of an ambulance. Their heads tilted inward, arms crossed tightly over their chests. Kara had begged him not to give chase until he'd had his burns looked at, but Ryder hadn't felt them then. All he'd been able to think of was getting his hands on Sand. He'd been so close that he could almost feel his fingers tightening the handcuffs around Sand's wrists.

Kara's face was the first to lift from the huddle. Her gaze found Ryder immediately. Deep lines cut across her forehead and gathered between her brows as she watched him draw nearer. "You shouldn't have left on your own again."

Ryder disagreed. No one else had been there to follow Sand, and someone had to. Time was everything, and there was none to spare.

"You look like hell," Uncle Henry said in lieu of "Hello."

Ryder hadn't exactly taken time to look in a mirror yet, but judging by the missing skin on his hand and searing pain in his face with every whisper of wind, he believed him.

"He just ran off like that," Kara complained, waving a hand as if to showcase his injuries. "The minute the worst of the explosion settled, he was out of the truck and racing into the smoke."

Ryder had raced into the thicket of trees outside his old neighborhood and across a small stream on the other side. He'd hoped to catch a glimpse of Sand, or at least find a clue about the direction in which he'd fled, but there was nothing. No tracks in the parched earth. No broken limbs or thudding footfalls. "I thought I could at least see which way he went or what kind of vehicle he was driving."

Uncle Henry moved cautiously toward him, a pile of unopened bandages in one hand and some kind of plastic bottle in the other. "I need to clean those wounds."

Cole and Kara locked him in serious stares.

Ryder didn't have the energy left to argue, and the burns were starting to hurt. "We can't reach Mom and Dad. Someone needs to check on Casey." The thought had sickened him every step of his way through the old neighborhood in search of Sand. "We don't know where Sand went, and Mom and Dad weren't answering their phones when we tried calling them earlier."

Kara set a small hand on his elbow. "West's spoken with them. They're okay."

He slumped against the silver bumper of Uncle Henry's bus and rolled his shoulders. Injured, angry and shaken to his core, Ryder wanted nothing more than to get back out there and search for Sand. But it was time to step back and evaluate how this day had gone so wrong.

He'd been so certain he had Sand right where he'd wanted him, that he'd run full speed toward a car bomb and had had no idea. Ryder had been so focused on catching Sand that he hadn't stopped to wonder *why Sand had indulged in all the theatrics.*

Why would Sand call Kara's landline? Why would he lead them into a purposeless ambush of tiny bottle bombs just to run away and jump into his car? Why would a clever criminal ever intentionally let him know what he was driving?

He wouldn't, and he didn't. It wasn't his car. It had been a trap, and Ryder had walked, no, *he'd run*, right into it.

Timothy Sand had plans stacked ten deep, and Ryder just kept signing up to be his puppet.

"Ow!" He jerked away from Uncle Henry. "Dammit!"

Henry slapped his hand away. "Be still." He ripped the packaging on a sterile bandage, then placed the clean white square gently against Ryder's jaw. "These are second-degree burns. You're going to need to keep them clean and covered for a couple weeks at least, maybe more than three. Depends."

He leveled Ryder with a no-nonsense stare. "What happened here?"

Ryder grimaced. "Arson."

Uncle Henry shook his head slowly. "That's what you said last time. You're going to tell me this is arson on your chin?"

"Might be a bit of chemical burns, too," Ryder admitted. "He threw a Molotov cocktail at my head. I blocked it with my hand."

Uncle Henry gave a sour look. "And your face. Let me see your hands."

Ryder lifted the one he'd used to thwart the attack.

Uncle Henry repeated the careful cleaning and bandaging process he'd performed on Ryder's jaw and cheek.

Cole lifted a palm in goodbye. "I was just here for muscle in case you tried to get away without having those burns treated. Now I'm going to help canvass Kara's neighborhood. See what turns up."

Ryder waited impatiently for Uncle Henry to stop fussing with him, then dragged himself back onto his feet and winced at the pain. "Thanks."

"Don't mention it. Though if you need me again tomorrow, I might start charging you a frequent-flier rate."

Ryder walked away, waving a hand overhead. "I've got calls to make." First to his parents, then to his team. He needed to check on Casey before he did anything else.

Behind him, Uncle Henry delivered verbal instructions for the care and treatment of Ryder's burns. "Everything you need is in the bag," he said. "Call me if he gives you any trouble."

Ryder climbed behind the wheel of his dad's truck, aching to scream until the hills fell down around him. Kara wasn't his caregiver. He didn't need a nurse, or a bagful of pills and bandages. He needed Sand hogtied and tossed in the back of the burnt-up pickup.

KARA FASTENED HER safety belt, then jammed the bag of medical supplies into the glove box. It'd been more than an hour since she'd saved Ryder from being blown to pieces by the car bomb, but her heart still raced like it was happening again and again.

"Call Mom," Ryder said, shifting into Drive. His tone and expression were hard, challenging. His gaze was distant.

Kara had seen him look like that before. In fact, during the days preceding their breakup, Ryder had rarely looked any other way.

She watched him carefully as the phone rang, searching for signs he would be okay. Hoping for some measure of kindness or normalcy to return to him. She'd barely gotten him back, and she was losing him all over again. Fear and pain came clutching at her heart and clawing their ways into her mind.

You will never be enough for him.

There will always be another fugitive, another cause, another chase.

Casey deserves better than a man who's only half in.

"Ryder?" His mom's voice jumped through the speakers. "Are you okay? Your father and brothers have barely told me anything. Where are you? What can I do?"

He narrowed his eyes and repositioned his white-knuckled grip on the steering wheel. "We're on our way to you. How's Casey?"

Kara whipped her gaze to Ryder's stoic face. He was worried about Casey? Not thinking about

Sand? She stared at the nearest speaker, waiting for an answer.

Why hadn't his mother answered him yet?

Her heart rate sprinted impossibly faster. The only solace she'd had since the bottle bombs began coming was that knowing Sand was near her meant he wasn't near her baby.

A sudden sigh blew through the speakers. "Casey's wonderful, adorable and perfect," she answered. "How are *you*?"

Kara deflated. Casey was okay.

"I'm pissed," Ryder answered.

"Are you hurt?"

Ryder clenched and worked his jaw but didn't answer.

For a moment, Kara considered reaching for his hand the way he always reached for hers when she was in distress. The lethal expression on his face warned her off. Something more than worry was going on inside his head, and Kara didn't want to think about the truth of that.

"We called earlier," Ryder snapped. "You didn't answer. Dad didn't answer. Why?"

"I don't know," she said. "The reception's not great here unless we're near the house or the road, but we took Casey to see the stables when we got here. She loved the horses. Was that when you called?"

Ryder looked thoroughly disgusted. "I thought something happened to you."

"No," she said with finality. "*We're* fine. *You* were hurt."

"Hi, Mrs. Garrett," Kara said, addressing his mother before Ryder said something rude that he would regret. No matter his mood, she owed his parents everything for keeping her baby safe. "Casey's doing okay?"

"Yes." Mrs. Garrett's voice was sweet but strained, and in that moment, Kara understood. Her earlier pause had nothing to do with a problem on her end and everything to do with fear for her baby: Ryder, the twenty-eight-year-old US marshal. He'd been in danger and he was hurt; so was his mother's heart by association. "I borrowed a swimsuit from Susie's granddaughter for Casey, and she's been splashing her little hands in a basin of water for a long while now. Cries when we take it away. She'll be happy until lunchtime."

The bud of a smile crested Kara's lips. Casey wasn't even wearing that dress and booties anymore.

Sand really couldn't see her. He wasn't magical. He was one man who could only be one place at a time.

And he wasn't with her baby.

RYDER CROSSED THE bridge over the river and forced his thoughts away from Sand. Obsessing was how he'd lost everything the first time around. He wouldn't let that happen again.

"Hey," he said, reaching for Kara's hand on the seat between them. "You okay?"

She chewed her bottom lip, staring intently through the passenger window. "No," she said flatly. She swiveled occasionally as if she'd seen something significant pass by. "I keep thinking I see him."

Ryder knew that feeling well.

He checked his rearview for signs of a tail, then pressed the gas pedal a little harder beneath the toe of his boot.

Kara shifted nervous blue eyes to him, then back to her window. "I hate that he's brought Casey into this. She's a baby, and he knows by now that she isn't yours, so what's his point?"

Ryder ignored the punch to his chest. Casey wasn't his, but he wanted her to be. "He wants to punish me."

How could Kara ever allow Ryder to be in her baby's life when he'd put her in danger before they'd even met? The invisible fist twisted against his sternum, stealing his air and delivering a powerful realization. Ryder didn't want to just be *in* Casey's life, like a neighbor or a family friend. He wanted to be *part* of her life. *Part of her family.* The revelation would have been enough to knock him down if he wasn't already seated.

"How can anyone want to hurt a baby?" Kara continued, still watching for signs of Sand at every turn.

Ryder cleared his throat and squeezed her hand. Oxygen seemed to return to his lungs when she opened her palm to him and twined their fingers.

"His games are about hurting me. Not you. You're going to be okay," Ryder said.

He willed the words to be true, but even as he spoke them, they rang false in his mind.

"Really?" Kara's voice hitched an octave. "He murdered his ex-wife's entire family, the Sayers family, and I don't even know how many others. He hurt their children. What makes you think he won't hurt mine?"

Ryder flinched. Jennifer Sayers had answered his questions and helped Ryder locate Sand. She should have been the hero of that story, but instead she'd been murdered for her good deeds, and Ryder would never shake the feeling it was partially his fault she and her family were gone.

"Sand is a psychopath," he said, rubbing a heavy hand against his aching eyes. "He's cold-blooded, but he's never killed anyone who didn't cross him first." Sand was meticulous and calculating, but never erratic. "His ex-wife ran from him. Her family hid her from him. Jennifer Sayers helped me find him. You and Casey have done nothing to him."

Kara pulled her hand free and waved it in the air. "I haven't wronged him? I called West and filed a report after he scared me at the park. I went to the sheriff's department and gave the media his current description. Was that any less than what he punished Jennifer Sayers and her entire family for?"

The truth hit Ryder and splintered like a thousand ice slivers down his spine. He wasn't alone on Sand's hit list, and Kara wasn't just a means to rattle Ryder. Kara had earned herself a place on that list, too.

And little Casey had everything to lose.

Chapter Thirteen

Kara unbuckled her seat belt and powered her window down as the truck rolled along an unfamiliar dirt driveway. Aunt Susie's small Craftsman-style home sprouted from behind a grove of apple trees. The world there was painfully still. No vehicles in sight. No signs of Mr. or Mrs. Garrett, Casey or Aunt Susie. Not even a dog raced over the land to bark at the newcomers.

"It's so quiet," Kara said, fear climbing over her skin. "What if something's wrong?"

Ryder opened his mouth to speak, but the sound of an approaching engine spun her in her seat.

A whoosh of relief flew from her lungs at the sight of Mr. Garrett on a four-wheeler behind them. A shotgun rode across the vehicle's handlebars, secured in a custom rack.

She tapped anxious fingers on the door at her side as Ryder pulled the truck around back. His dad passed them, angling his four-wheeler through the grass and parking outside a massive structure at the rear of the property. He dismounted his ride, then opened a set of barn doors tall and wide enough to guide an airplane inside. Kara's hand slid eagerly into position around the handle.

Ryder parked his dad's torched-up truck beside his mom's Ford.

Kara was out and moving toward Mr. Garrett before Ryder settled the engine.

"She's in the house," Mr. Garrett said as she drew nearer, but his eyes were fixed over her shoulder on his injured son.

Kara broke into a sprint, headed for the home's back door. She knocked hastily before dashing inside, unwilling to stay away a moment longer for the sake of manners. "Hello?"

A portly gray-haired woman peeped her head through an interior doorway. "Kara Noble?"

Kara's headed bobbed wildly. "Yes. I'm so sorry. I didn't mean to be rude, I'm just…" Her voice cracked, and a bolt of emotion struck through her. "Is Casey here?"

The woman stepped fully into sight then, a shotgun in her left hand. She extended her right. "Of course. It's nice to meet you. I'm Aunt Susie. Your little angel is right through here."

Kara shook Aunt Susie's hand, then followed on her heels. They wound through the open archways of several small rooms, all delightfully warm and welcoming, before arriving at their destination.

Mrs. Garrett sat in a rocking chair with a sleeping Casey cradled against her chest. A beach towel speckled with rubber ducks was draped neatly over them both. "Wore herself out," she said proudly. "This one loves the water."

"May I?" Kara asked, moving in close and reaching for her daughter. She turned Casey's limp body around and cuddled her against her heart, then collapsed onto the nearby couch in sheer bliss.

Kara stroked her daughter's hair and lowered her nose to inhale the sweet scent of her skin. She kissed each of Casey's tiny dimpled fingers before pressing her perfect palm against her cheek. Kara's eyelids slid shut, and she felt peaceful and complete. In that moment, there was no danger outside, no spectators inside, only her and Casey. Nothing else mattered and things were right again with the world.

The back door opened and shut again, jarring Kara's eyes open.

"Don't shoot," Mr. Garrett said playfully, his hands raised in mock surrender.

Aunt Susie lowered her rifle.

Ryder moved into the room with a deep frown. "Cole says there was a report of someone fitting Sand's description in my parents' neighborhood this morning. A jogger stopped by the sheriff's department to let us know he saw him three hours ago. As if that is somehow helpful now." Anger scorched a path over Ryder's cheeks. "Not sure how I'm supposed to catch him three hours ago, but at least we can confirm the theory Sand only had Casey in his sights while we were all together. Once we split up, he had to make a choice. He chose us."

"He got away again," Kara said. "Are we sure he didn't follow us here?" She whispered the words, but inside her head she was screaming. Could Sand be out there? Lurking just beyond the walls of Aunt Susie's cozy home? If no one knew where he was, how could anyone be sure he hadn't circled around and followed them there? "We could've led him right here."

Ryder lowered his lean frame onto the couch at her side, his pain and fatigue as evident as his disappointment. "He didn't follow us. I was very careful."

Mr. Garrett moved to the armchair across from them. "What's your next move?"

"I don't know." Ryder dropped his head back and stared at the ceiling, as if the answers were written there. "He's escalating," he said. "He used to be satisfied taunting me. Today, he tried to kill me." Ryder lifted his face. His bandages were dark and needed to be changed. "He's planned it all out. He bought the explosives a week ago." Ryder leaned forward, bracing both elbows against his thighs and gripping his head in one hand. "He didn't come here to continue our game. He came to end it."

Mrs. Garrett stood on shaky legs and moved toward the kitchen. "I'm going to pour some sweet tea and fix a snack."

Mr. Garrett kept his eyes on Ryder. "Your murder is the agenda now."

"Apparently."

"Well, that changes things for the worse. Did you hear about the online money trail your team is following?"

"Yeah," Ryder frowned. "He bought C-4. We just saw it in action."

His dad glanced from Ryder to Kara. "According to West, Sand also bought enough incendiaries and propellants to light up Kentucky, and we're going on thirty-three days with no rain."

Ryder clenched and released his good fist. "I'm worried he's had some kind of mental break. The escalation feels sudden and extreme."

Kara waited to catch Ryder's eye. "He could've been planning this a long while. Maybe the whole time he was on probation. Maybe longer. What's sudden to you might have been a slow unraveling for him." She planted a kiss on her baby's face and tried to stay calm. She'd nearly seen Ryder blown to bits today, and the image of him running toward the bomb hadn't stopped replaying in her mind. What would have happened if West hadn't warned her? If she hadn't gotten to him soon enough? Would Sand have left town, satisfied, or would he have kept coming for her and Casey until they were all reduced to smoke and ashes? She couldn't bear to think of it. "Maybe I should take Casey away for a while. Hop on a plane and just go. Sand might be easier to find if he's looking for two people who've left the continent. I've always wanted to visit Timbuktu."

Mr. Garrett snorted. "You'll have to buy three tickets. I don't think you'll be able to separate my wife from your baby."

As if on cue, Mrs. Garrett returned with a tray and a smile. Five glasses and a pitcher of sweet tea sat beside a big plate of cubed cheese, fruit and crackers. Crisp wedges of vegetables were piled along the plates' sides. "Help yourselves."

Mr. Garrett patted his middle, quickly moving toward the tray. "Nervous cooker. She loves us with food."

Ryder sucked down a glass of tea without stopping, wiped the back of one hand across his brow then poured a second glass.

"Are you okay?" Kara asked. She'd never seen Ryder look so wrecked. "You should take the pills Henry gave you for pain. I put them in the glove box."

"I will." He rocked onto one hip and freed his cell phone. "It's Cole." He hit the speaker button and palmed the device, making it easier for the entire room to hear. "Garrett."

"Hey," Cole began. "Where are you?"

"With Mom and Dad."

Kara glanced at their blessed hostess. Ryder's gaze was on her, too. He'd intentionally omitted her name.

Aunt Susie watched silently from the room's corner, shotgun within reaching distance. Her gray hair was wound into a tight bun at the nape of her neck, and her clothes were neat as a pin, but something about her quiet disposition assured she could handle herself, whatever came.

Ryder dropped his attention back to the phone. "What do you have?"

"I got a call from a local gas station attendant who thinks Sand was in there thirty minutes ago. She sent some stills from the station's surveillance footage of a man fitting his description, but he's got a ball cap pulled low over his forehead in the picture, and his shoulders are hunched. Hard to say for sure if it's him. Even his exact height and build are hard to determine in the photos. I think it's worth checking out."

"What's he driving?" Ryder asked.

"Looks like a late-model hatchback. Possibly foreign. I'm headed over there now to interview the clerk and see the video footage firsthand. I thought you might want to meet me there."

"Give me thirty minutes," Ryder said, pushing back onto his feet. "We're going to need to relocate the clerk when we finish. Put her up somewhere outside the county for a few nights. I'll alert my team we've got an immediate witness in need of concealment."

His gravelly voice and ruddy cheeks broke Kara's heart. Jennifer Sayers was a clerk who'd helped him, too, once, and look how that had turned out.

He stuffed the phone back into his pocket and reached for Kara. "Walk me out?"

She let him pull her up, careful not to disturb Casey. Much as she hated to risk waking the baby, she refused to miss the chance to say goodbye to Ryder.

He shook his dad's hand, then kissed his mother and Aunt Susie on their cheeks. "I'll be in touch when I know something."

His mom nodded bravely. "Be careful."

Inside the giant barn, Ryder turned to face Kara. "I know more about Sand's agenda now," he said, motioning to his burned face with his bandaged hand. "After what happened today, there's no doubt he'll kill me if I let him. I won't let him."

Kara did her best to maintain a strong front like his mother had, but she was new to this, and her composure was all but gone at the thought of losing him.

Ryder lifted his hand to cradle her chin and pierced her with sincere eyes. "I will come back to you."

"Promise."

He lowered his gaze to her lips. "Always."

Ryder wound his injured hand behind her back and pulled her closer with his forearm, until their bodies aligned, toes to waist.

Casey snored gently between them, completely unaffected by the dangers of her world.

Ryder kissed Casey's head. He traced her round cheek with careful fingertips, then raised his eyes to her mother. "I will protect her."

Kara blinked tear-filled eyes. "Kiss me goodbye?" she asked softly.

A pleased moan rumbled in his chest, and he planted a powerful kiss on Kara's mouth.

Her limbs went light and her head went fuzzy. It was the kind of kiss she wanted to wake up and fall asleep to every day for the rest of her life.

He released her too soon and onto unsteady feet. "That wasn't goodbye."

She lifted her fingertips to still-tingling lips and watched as his truck's taillights disappeared down the driveway. She wanted desperately to believe that Ryder would choose her over Timothy Sand if it came down to that again. Not just for her and Casey, but for Ryder. The last time, his obsession had left him broken. This time it could get him killed.

WEST AND COLE were already at the gas station when Ryder arrived. The clerk was young and happy. She seemed genuinely thrilled to be useful in the search for Timothy Sand, and it broke Ryder's heart. She had no clue what that report could cost her.

"Thank you," Ryder said when she finished. "Two members of my team will be here shortly to escort you to your home. You'll have some time to pack your things and make a few calls, then you'll be escorted outside the county and kept safe until we find the arsonist you saw in here today."

Her proud expression turned to shock. "Am I in danger?"

Ryder nodded. "Yes. This man knows exactly who he's seen or spoken with, and he will know who helped us catch up with him." He fought to ignore the boulder of emotion resting on his windpipe. "We can keep you safe if you follow the marshals' instructions. Witness protection is a service we take seriously and do very well."

Her eyes widened, and color bled from her skin. "Witness protection?"

Cole shot Ryder an ugly look, then reached for the girl. "Come on. He means well, but he's intense."

The clerk toddled along behind him, dumbfounded and tossing stray looks over her shoulder to Ryder as they exited the building.

West clapped him on the back. "Well, that girl will never sleep again."

Ryder stretched his neck. "What else can I do? Where's the line?" he asked. "What is the right amount of advice and honesty that makes folks pay attention, but won't scare them half to death? This *is* scary. And it's life or death."

West shrugged. "I don't know. I'm just saying she's calling her therapist right now. That's all."

Ryder shook his hands out hard at the wrists, trying to dislodge the tension that seemed to encase his body like iron. "What are you doing over there?" He moved toward West and the mess he had spread on the countertop.

West turned a wad of messy papers toward him. "Credit card receipts."

"He wouldn't pay with a credit card," Ryder scoffed. "He hasn't held a job for more than a few months in over a decade, and credit cards are traceable. He's not stupid, and this isn't his first rodeo."

West pressed a receipt against Ryder's chest. "Oh, yeah?"

Ryder lifted the paper into view. The signature was nothing but a scribble and a long flat line. "What's it say?"

"Credit card fraud. That card belongs to Mr. Bradly Perkins, a man who happened to file a report this afternoon about his late-model hatchback that was stolen last night from the Hitchin' Post Saloon. His wallet was in the glove box. When I got the report this morning, I figured Mr. Perkins could get in line for the department's attention. Killer arsonist on the loose and all. I didn't have a spare officer to search for his car, which I assumed was probably still parked at his friend's house or along the street somewhere. Mr. Perkins was nursing a heavy hangover when he called. I told him we'd get to it as soon as we were able. Then I started thinking, we don't get a lot of car thefts around here, and I wondered if anyone in Cade County might be in need of a new ride and a stolen identity. Guess who came to mind."

A small smile curled Ryder's mouth. He freed his phone from his pocket and swiped the screen to life. "You're a genius, brother."

"Yeah, but you can call me Sheriff."

Ryder pressed the phone to his ear.

Ten minutes later, tech support had provided the

most recent activity on Mr. Bradly Perkins's stolen Mastercard.

Ryder scrolled carefully through the text message, searching for a clue to Sand's whereabouts. He read one line twice, and a smile broke across his lips. "Gotcha."

West angled around for a better look at the little screen. "Well, looky there. Mr. Perkins checked into a hotel around lunchtime today. Wonder if that was before or after he filed the report?"

"Can't say," Ryder mused. "Could be a trap."

"Could be the break we need." West tidied his mess, then stopped to speak with Cole and the clerk on his way out.

Ryder hoped West was right because Ryder sure didn't want to be this time.

A black SUV pulled into the lot at Cole's side. Two US Marshals climbed out, ready to protect the girl.

She turned the lights out and flipped the sign in the window to Closed before returning to the somber-faced men trading supportive nods with Ryder. They would take care of her. Ryder didn't have to worry. He could put everything he had into the much larger problem at hand. Like a plan to capture Sand when he returned to the hotel. Ryder needed to set up an ambush and bring Sand in without anyone else getting hurt. Or killed.

West and Cole pointed their cruisers onto the

road, and Ryder shifted into Drive behind them. Next stop: the Lucky A Hotel.

THE GARRETTS PULLED into the restaurant parking lot beside the hotel and fell into formation on the pavement. Ryder took point, flanked by his brothers.

A blast of icy air poured over his shoulders as he entered the main office through a side door. Cole and West stood outside, keeping watch for signs of Sand.

A cranky-looking redhead glared at Ryder from behind the desk. Her pointed gaze fell to the shiny star hanging from a beaded metal chain around his neck. "Yeah?"

He forced a tight smile, recalling his mother's theory that it was easier to catch bees with honey than vinegar. "Hello, ma'am. I'm US Marshal Ryder Garrett. I'd like to ask you a couple questions about a man staying here."

"Pft." She turned her face away, returning her attention to the daytime talk show playing on her rabbit-eared TV.

He strode to the desk, pressing forward until his toes hit the cheap wooden veneer. "Excuse me?"

She rolled her eyes. "I ain't allowed to give out information on our guests. That's invasion of privacy."

Ryder clenched his jaw until he thought his teeth would snap. "Please don't misunderstand. I have reason to believe a very dangerous man is staying at your hotel. My need to apprehend him supersedes your need to protect his privacy."

She didn't look convinced. "I think you need a warrant."

"I don't…" He raised his palms in exasperation, then marched around the desk and bumped her out of the way. A few keystrokes and mouse clicks later, Ryder had what he'd come for. "Thank you." He gave her a limp salute on his way out.

The woman tapped frantically on her phone, a fierce scowl on her face as she watched him leave.

"Come on," he told his brothers as the door swung shut behind him. "Room 117."

They moved swiftly along the hotel's exterior wall, making their way to Sand's room.

West checked his phone and snorted. "Dispatch says there's someone at this hotel harassing staff and posing as a marshal."

Ryder shot him a sour look, then pointed to a white hatchback up ahead.

Cole ducked to the car's side and set his palm to the hood. "Still warm."

"Television's on," West reported, standing just outside the room in question.

A thrill of victory ignited Ryder's cache of adrenaline. He circled a finger in the air, instructing his brothers to cover all the exit points, then pulled out his cell phone and called his team. They needed backup to contain the situation and a bomb-sniffing dog to evaluate the perimeter before Ryder kicked the door down.

Timothy Sand was about to get a brand-new jail cell with free rent for life.

Chapter Fourteen

Room 117 was surrounded. Just twenty minutes after Ryder's call, every spare lawman in Cade County was in place, including four tightly wound Garretts ready to put Timothy Sand behind bars.

"One," Ryder mouthed, taking position in front of the door.

A plain-clothed deputy had walked a bomb-sniffing dog past the door twice, playing the role of bored animal-owner, allowing the canine time to scent for explosives.

"Two." To Ryder's surprise, the door wasn't booby trapped.

He waited one beat longer, then kicked the door down, three years of frustration fueling his aggression. He marched inside, gun drawn. "US marshal." He moved swiftly room to room, clearing the messy space with a pack of reinforcements behind him.

Two additional marshals had made the trip to Shadow Point from Cincinnati following the car bomb, and they'd arrived in time to join the capture team. A stroke of much-needed luck after losing the other two to protect the clerk.

Unfortunately, this was no longer a corner-and-capture mission.

This was another miss.

"Clear," he said one final time, feeling his hopeful heart turn slowly to stone. Ryder holstered his sidearm and let loose a slew of swears, forcing himself not to topple something or kick the wall.

Behind him, the explosives dog barked, commanding the room's attention and directing it to a set of empty duffel bags and suitcases stacked inside the closet.

Blake pulled free of the cluster of lawmen, his FBI badge gleaming under the cheap fluorescent lights, and went to get a closer look.

The marshals descended on a small round table covered in photographs and newspaper articles.

An entourage of men and women in a mix of plain clothes and uniforms gathered outside the open door, speaking to other hotel guests and making guesses as to how Timothy Sand had made another clever escape.

Ryder imagined screaming, swearing and pounding something until the excess energy, anger and adrenaline were spilled from him, but there was no time for that. No time to waste on outbursts and tantrums. It was time to double down. Make his own plan and get his priorities in order.

West appeared in his periphery, breaking through

the crowded room in a straight line to Ryder's side. "You okay?"

"Yep."

"You sure, cause you look like you're about to lose your mind."

"Yep."

West gave him a long once-over, cocked hip, tipped head, scrutinizing eyes. "My guys are going to canvass the area. See if anyone saw Sand today, which way he went, anything like that." He glanced over his shoulder at Blake, who was frowning into empty bags and suitcases. "Looks like he was holding a lot of nasty materials in here. Nasty, *flammable* materials. I'm hoping he used all the C-4 in the car. I don't want to think about what else he has in mind."

Ryder rubbed his brows. "Any use hoping that was his big play, and he botched my murder, so he's out of moves?"

Blake shook his head. "Nah."

"Garrett." A marshal Ryder knew as Jim Riggs waved from the table covered in newspaper clippings and photographs.

The Garrett brothers circled him at the little table.

Ryder was sure Jim had only meant to get *his* attention, but calling out for "Garrett" in Shadow Point rarely turned up fewer than two or three responders. "What've you got?" Ryder asked, staring at piles of sorted photos.

The marshal looked from brother to brother as the Garretts closed in around him. "I know y'all are brothers, but I don't think I've ever seen four people look so much alike."

"Jim?" Ryder pushed, redirecting the man's commentary. "You found something you want me to see?"

"Sorry. It's just really weird," he muttered under his breath. "Here." He turned a stack of papers to face the Garretts. "These are all articles and photos of you from the last three years. Everything's date-stamped, like he was chronicling your life, and he's stalked your career pretty tightly, too, especially the last twelve months."

Ryder lifted the nearest stack of evidence and flipped through the unnerving pages.

"I sorted all the piles by date," Jim said. "You've got the most recent. They get older moving left to right."

West chose the pile closest to him and thumbed through the photos. He let out a long, slow whistle. "This is all from those first days when you left town. You looked like hell. He tracked your fall from grace damn closely. Probably wore it like a feather in his cap."

Ryder examined the collection in his hand. "I can't let him take all the credit."

Ryder had chosen to chase the monster at the expense of everything else.

Not this time.

Ryder cringed at first sight of the final photo in his stack. A snapshot of him taken in the last forty-eight hours, since his return to Shadow Point. Sand had drawn a big sad face on his lips and put neat X's over his eyes. The repetitive arch and curve of pen-drawn flames bordered the page's edge. He stood outside the sheriff's department in the photo.

Cole walked away. "This guy's sick." He appraised the room for a long beat before he began running his hands along the hanging photos. "He left plenty of his crazy out in the open. Let's see what he's hiding." He moved on to peering inside the vents with a flashlight.

West lifted another stack of papers. "And here we have a detailed account of your more recent rise to fame."

Jim snorted.

Ryder grunted. He was hardly famous, but he knew what West saw. "I was only standing in."

West turned an article in Ryder's direction, misplaced pride all over his face. "You led Ohio's most successful drug task force in the state's history? Last fall?"

Ryder shrugged. "They needed a warm body. I was between witness relocations, and I run a steady ninety-eight-point-six. I qualified."

"Sure," West said. "No big deal." He made a crazy face and turned back to the stacks of papers. "You've got to call home more."

Ryder didn't deserve any accolades for his work as a lawman. He'd been stalked for three years without a single clue it was happening. That took an amazing lack of skills. Sand had been in Cincinnati with him. Bought copies of the local newspaper detailing his career drama. Hell, he'd probably even watched Ryder drive haplessly to work every day. *At the US Marshals office.* All while he took his picture.

Cole gave up on the vents and knelt beside the bed, gloved hands searching busily between the mattress and box springs. "Bingo." When he stood, he had a notebook in his hand.

Ryder moved to his side. "What's that? Is it Sand's?"

Cole lifted and dropped a noncommittal shoulder. "Someone doodled a stick figure with X's on his eyes and flames on his head. Big star on his chest. Put it right here on the cover." He held the notebook up beside Ryder's head.

Blake laughed.

Ryder snatched the notebook from him. He turned the pages slowly, mesmerized and horrified by the heavy-handed scrawls. "It's all nonsense. It says, 'Stop following me. Let me live. Stop following me. Go away. Go away. Go away.'" He frowned at the little book, wishing he could throw it through the window. "Is this a joke? A planted thing to make me chase my tail some more?"

Another clue that meant nothing, led nowhere. Just like all the others.

Cole craned his neck and read over Ryder's shoulder. "I didn't think that guy could get any creepier. I was wrong."

West reached for the book. "May I?" He looked stricken as he turned the pages. "Those words and phrases sound like pleas. They aren't aggressive like the photographs, though that spectacular rendering on the cover is a little worrisome." He flipped back to the stick-figure marshal. "I'd say the nut is coming fully unhinged. But we already knew that. What do you think about me asking my wife to weigh in on this? Unofficially." His jaw went rigid, his eyes, hard. "She's a clinical psychologist with some recent and very personal experience in handling stalkers."

"Yeah," Ryder agreed. "If she's willing. I'll take whatever edge I can get. This is new territory for me." West's wife, Tina, had undergone a horrible ordeal when her stalker stole her baby and tried to force Tina into a weird mommy-and-daddy relationship with him. She'd been lucky to get out with her life. West had played a major role in that, but he didn't like to talk about it.

Ryder nudged West with his elbow and nodded his appreciation. He was lucky to have brothers like his most days. But especially this one.

Blake turned his phone's camera on the notebook as West flipped the pages. "This can't be good," he said. "The guy stalks you for three years, then fills his creepy little notebook with pleas for someone to stop following him?" He raised an eyebrow.

It didn't make any sense to Ryder, either, but Sand had never been sane to start with. "Being on the run wears on a person," he said. "I see it in the witnesses I relocate. They've sometimes been underground for ages before they come forward and ask for protection. Hiding always seems to chip away at their sanity. Makes them paranoid and constantly on edge. The life he had while I was chasing him couldn't have been easy, especially for someone already so messed up, but this last year should have been better. The marshal's office caught him, tried him and let him go with a temporary ankle bracelet." Ryder felt his muscles tighten. Sand had killed entire families, but he'd avoided jail time, and now he got to walk free.

Blake scrolled through the photos of the notebook on his phone. "I can't say I feel sorry for a flame-throwing murderer, but I wouldn't mind helping end the man's life on the run. Maybe tuck him into a tidy little cell at the local penitentiary for a hundred or so years."

"That's the goal," Ryder said. He checked his watch for the tenth time. Hours had passed since he'd left Kara and Casey at Aunt Susie's, and Kara was probably thinking the worst.

He scanned the room, deliberating. He could stay and help tear the hotel apart looking for Sand, the little cockroach, maybe hunt for clues, go door-to-door canvassing with the deputies, or sit tight and pore over the stalker-grade surveillance photos on the table until he lost his mind, or he could go to Kara.

He was done with choosing work over family.

Ryder had a lady and a baby to protect, and the

former was probably worried sick. Kara and Casey might not be Ryder's by marriage or blood, but his heart had laid a heavy claim to them, and his mind was working on how to make it official. "Let me know what else you find. I'm going to get Dad on the road with the girls. Wherever Sand is, he's got his hands full trying not to be identified by the horde of lawmen on his tail and most of Shadow Point on the lookout. This is the perfect time to move Kara and Casey to the next location. I'll meet them there."

"Cabin?" Blake asked.

Ryder gave a stiff dip of his chin.

"That's good." Blake said. "Off the grid. Virtually unused. And not easy to get to. Wherever Sand is, he left his car out front. He might see you pull out of here, but he can only follow you so far before his legs get tired."

Ryder said his goodbyes, then jumped in the truck, eager to arrive physically where his heart had been all day.

KARA SAT ON the small front porch of an old log cabin in the mountains near the national park. The land had been in the Garrett family since before the park was anything more than the local hunting grounds. The cabin had been built by their ancestors' hands. Somehow it wasn't a hard stretch of her imagination to see any of the Garrett men living in the rustic home today.

Mr. Garrett sat a few feet away, perched on the

steps, shotgun balanced across his thighs as he whittled something from a fallen branch he'd cracked over one knee and busted into a wedge the size of a coffee mug. "Someone's coming," he said, setting the knife and piece of wood aside, then taking up his rifle. "Better see who it is."

Apparently his superhuman hearing didn't come with an ability to see the future.

Kara stilled, but Casey didn't notice. Snuggled warmly against her mama's chest and tummy, Casey's tiny mouth moved in sweet little circles as she dreamed of an invisible bottle, no doubt. For a moment, Kara wondered if she should wait inside the cabin until the guest arrived, or maybe even prepare to run. Mr. Garrett had promised her they weren't followed, but she wasn't feeling very secure anywhere today.

Rifle in hand, Mr. Garrett moved silently along the path covered with twigs and leaves that he called a road. He stopped at the crest of the hill and raised his arm to whatever he saw beyond.

Kara had no idea what it meant. A greeting? A warning? Hopefully it wasn't her signal to run. Though, if she had to flee, she knew what she'd do. It was the only thing she could think of since arriving at the cabin with her baby.

First, Kara would run behind the cabin and over the hill. If she kept moving down the slope long enough, eventually she'd come to the river that ran along the docks at the edge of town. Then, she could follow the racing water back to civilization.

She knew better than to try to make it back on her own by wandering in the woods. Everything looked exactly the same on the mountain. Brown mud and twigs and tree trunks. A thick green canopy overhead. Fallen leaves from seasons long past clung to the earthen floor.

Mr. Garrett moved again, this time into the tree line, an expectant look on his brow.

Ryder's SUV rocked into view, bouncing over the pitted remnants of a long-forgotten road. She was somehow thankful he'd left his dad's truck with the burnt-up bed behind.

Her heart leaped at the sight of him climbing down from behind the wheel. She ached to run to him, to embrace him and to cry relieved tears of joy and thankfulness, but she contained herself, determined to keep her escalated emotions in check. She settled for allowing her smile to spread widely and enjoyed the relief as her limbs grew lighter with the knowledge that Ryder was okay.

He was better than okay. He was there.

Mr. Garrett hugged his son, then climbed into the driver's seat of Ryder's SUV. "Take good care of that baby," he said, shifting into reverse gear.

Kara lifted one hand in goodbye, surprised to see him go so soon. "Okay." The word came too late, and his taillights were already gone, rolling back from sight, down the long, questionable road to the busy town below.

Her attention jumped to the handsome US marshal moving confidently in her direction.

"Sorry it took me so long," Ryder said. His voice was so low and thick she couldn't help wondering if there was a much deeper meaning there.

"Were you able to finish whatever you wanted to get done?"

"No." He moved closer, watching her and Casey with a soft smile. "Everyone's got a job to do. They all have my number if anything comes up." He gripped her hips and leaned into her with a warm, contented smile.

"You just left?" she asked, warmth blooming in her chest. He'd chosen her and Casey when he'd just gotten a huge break in this case? She felt her lips curling into a broad, hopeful smile. "That's not at all like the marshal I was engaged to once." That man had been the last one to leave every crime scene involving Timothy Sand, and he'd brought all that he could home with him, so he could keep working until dawn.

"That man died of a broken heart," he said, tucking hair behind her ear and letting his fingertips trail over her neck.

Kara shivered. "If everyone has a job to do, how did you manage to get back here? What about your job?"

"Well," he began, his loving smile turning wolfish. "My main priority is taking care of you. So, unless you have an objection, I was thinking I'd like to get started."

"No." She smiled, enjoying this side of him, the side who could be both marshal and family man. "No objections here."

Ryder kissed her cheek, then looked at the sleeping baby snuggled between them. "How's Casey?" he asked, cupping the top of her little head in his hand, then planting a kiss on her as well.

"Tired," Kara admitted, easily speaking for the both of them. "Why don't I put her down? I set up her playpen in the small bedroom, and I made coffee."

Ryder followed her into the cabin and to the room where the playpen stood.

"Okay." Kara crept away from the makeshift crib, and looked to Ryder for a plan of action. "Coffee?"

Ryder shook his head. His brilliant blue eyes were dark with want and his hands took no time in finding purchase on her hips and hauling her close. "I don't ever want to lose you again," he said. His Adam's apple bobbed long and slow.

Kara's heart seemed to swell and stretch with a thousand things she wanted to say, but could never properly articulate. "Good because I don't want to let you go again. I shouldn't have let you go before."

Ryder dropped his forehead against hers in what looked to be a sigh of relief. "And Casey?" he asked. "I've put her in so much danger."

Kara rocked her body against his, arching her back and rolling onto her toes. She brushed her lips seductively across his, turning his words of worry into a deep guttural moan. "We forgive you," she whispered.

Ryder curled his strong arms around her back and pressed her more firmly against the lean, muscled length of him. He lowered his mouth over hers, and warmth flooded through her on contact. His kiss curled her toes, made her gasp and set her world on fire.

Her palm grazed the bandage at his jaw, and she pulled back, afraid to hurt him. "Is it painful?" she asked. "To kiss me?"

"All I ever want to do is kiss you," he said. "It's going to take more than that little burn to keep me from it."

Kara smiled. Her roaming fingertips found the hem of his shirt and peeled it over the top of his head before moving to the waistband of his pants. "How's your hand?"

His eyes widened for a moment, before his lids drooped slightly and his expression went dark and lust-driven. Kara had missed that look even more than she realized. Her skin snapped and tingled with excitement and memories of what she could expect to come next.

"My hand's excellent," he said with a grin. Then, he had her shirt off and lying with his on the floor a second later. The heated skin of his torso pressed to hers, scorched a path of desire through her middle.

"I need you," she whispered breathlessly into his

ear, catching the perfect lobe between her lips. Kara wanted Ryder every way she could have him, and she never wanted to let him go once he agreed.

Ryder swept her feet out from under her and carried her to the bedroom across the hall. He lowered her onto the bed and hovered over her, watching her squirm at first, then trailing hot kisses across her collarbone and into the valley between her breasts. His unbandaged hand found the button at the top of her shorts, and he raised his heated gaze to hers in question.

Kara's hand fell immediately on his, eager to get their bodies back together as soon as possible and preferably without the clothes. "Do you need help?" She smiled, certain that removing her pants with one hand would take far longer than she could stand to wait.

Ryder's dark eyes caught hers with a mischievous twinkle. "I don't, but you might when I'm finished with you."

"Hell." She flopped against the bed and let her hands fall overhead in delicious anticipation.

Ryder dragged her zipper low and slow, continuing his delivery of hot wet kisses until Kara was sure she would soon need help saying thank-you.

Chapter Fifteen

Casey's cries pulled Kara from bed an hour later, far sooner than she was ready to leave Ryder's side. She padded to the next room and scooped her princess from the playpen. Casey's complaints quickly turned to coos of love and playfulness. Kara reveled in the simple joy of moments like these.

She swayed gently, instinctually, to the music of her infant's sweet sounds, and embracing the utter joy still flowing through her heart at the day's satisfying turn of events. Kara had fully anticipated Ryder standing guard at the windows all night while she sat silent in rigid fear. She hadn't even considered he might be as ready as she was to make their reunion official. And she had to admit, making love to her personal hero sounded worlds better than sitting silently anywhere. Her smile grew, and she pressed her lips to Casey's head. Kara had everything she wanted inside these cabin walls, and despite the monster lurking beyond, she was happy.

She turned in search of somewhere to snuggle and rock her baby, and started as she saw Ryder leaning, shirtless and motionless, against the doorjamb. The top button on his jeans was still undone, begging her fingers to slide them off one more time.

He watched her closely, smiling warmly and thoroughly melting Kara's heart.

"You're great with her," he said. "I've seen mothers with babies before, but you and her? Something else entirely."

Kara felt a welcome blush on her cheeks. There was no higher compliment, really. "She's been my world for a long time now. She was my best friend even before she was born."

Ryder moved into the room and wrapped them in his arms. "I'm so sorry I wasn't here to see you pregnant, to watch you glow and to comfort you when you were scared or lonely." He pressed his cheek against the top of Kara's head. "And I hate that I wasn't in that delivery room to meet your baby with you." His warm voice was thick with regret. "I've missed way too much."

Kara pulled back to look into his glossy eyes. The love and admiration so evident in his words were just as clear in his emotional stare. Ryder didn't resent her for being with another man, nor for trying to move on or even for having a baby with someone so poorly chosen that he'd left her. Ryder only hated that he'd missed so much.

She ran a palm over his chest before raising it to his cheek. She wasn't normally prone to believing in fairy tales, but it occurred to her then that this was probably what people meant when they used the term *soul mates*. Because nothing else mattered. Not the past. Not the future. Only that they would be together. Everything else was irrelevant. And now they had a sweet baby girl to make their story all the more enchanting.

Ryder's phone buzzed in the pocket of his jeans, and he loosened his grip on them to check the screen. "West," he said, snapping into business mode. He kissed Kara's nose and backed away to take the call, leaning against the nearest wall instead of walking out the door.

Kara appreciated that more than she could say. She basked in the feel of his eyes on her as she changed Casey's diaper and carried her into the kitchen for a bottle.

Ryder followed, copping a feel as she strode by.

Kara jumped and laughed, enjoying the little break from reality more than she should. The knowledge that playtime would soon end, possibly in catastrophe, niggled, ever present in the back of her mind. But all she could do was take the passing seconds as they came, and pray she was wrong about the catastrophe.

Kara unloaded the makings of a bottle onto the kitchen counter and began to mix the formula for Casey's next meal.

The house had been dusty from disuse when Kara had arrived with Mr. Garrett, but she'd put her nervous energy to use on the details. Now, everything smelled like lemons and evergreens. She'd scrubbed the place down and opened the windows, bringing the gorgeous summer day inside. She'd removed sheets from the furniture. Swept the floors. Wiped the counters. Then, moved on to the bedroom where everything she'd needed to turn the simple mattress and headboard into a cozy cabin bed had been carefully stowed in plastic bins and stacked in a closet. As a blessed bonus for her efforts, the coffee maker was in good working order.

"Nah," Ryder answered West's unheard question. His blue eyes sought hers, and she couldn't miss the impish glint. "I've brought her here before."

Kara smiled.

She and Ryder had come to the cabin to celebrate the one-month anniversary of their first date. He'd told her they were going to look at the stars, but in reality, they'd spent the night exploring one another.

It was her first time, and it had been one worth having. She'd always cherished the memory. No regrets about any bumbling high school sweetheart or a groping college frat boy. Just Kara, Ryder and his heartrending touch.

Ryder had been the town playboy, like his brothers before and after him. He'd sworn the rumors weren't true, but his experience was hard to deny once he'd gotten his hands on her. The temptation to give herself to a man had never even registered until Ryder. From the moment she'd first realized she loved him, Kara had needed him like she needed oxygen, and

the three years they'd spent apart had been as un-
fulfilling and uncomfortable as having never taken
a full breath.

"I guess I'm going to need a shirt," he said, tucking the cell phone safely away and moving in her direction, completely unaware of the lovely memories
she'd been reliving.

She pushed her bottom lip out and grazed the
backs of her fingertips over the smooth angles and
planes of his chest. "Are you leaving?" A pang of fear
pinched in her chest.

"No." He gave her a confident, cocky smile.
"Company's coming."

KARA WAITED IMPATIENTLY while Ryder dressed and
went to keep watch for Tina, West's wife. According to Ryder, Tina was a clinical psychologist they'd
brought into the loop on Sand, hoping she'd see
something in the evidence that they couldn't, like a
pattern that might help them figure out Sand's next
move. After reviewing the files, she'd requested an
audience with Ryder and Kara.

Kara's tummy twisted as she imagined what a
therapist would think of this man, and she was only
slightly certain she wanted to know what horrible
thing was going to happen next.

Ryder met Tina at the crest of the hill, the way his
dad had met him, but instead of taking her truck and
leaving, Ryder walked her to the porch and extended
his hand to introduce her. "This is Kara Noble. Kara,

my sister-in-law." He shot Tina a goofy smile. "Tina Garrett. Man, that never gets less weird."

She snorted. "Yeah? Have you ever been around when someone calls Rita 'Mrs. Cole Garrett?'"

Kara laughed with Ryder at that one. Little Cole Garrett was forever burned in everyone's minds as the baby brother of three rowdy troublemakers. He was Cole the middle school baseball star, and nobody thought of him as a veteran or a medic or a deputy, and certainly not a devoted, respectable husband. But there he was. All those things and still goofy as a three-legged pig.

Kara shook Tina's hand. "It's nice to meet you. This is my daughter, Casey."

Tina's smile softened and her face lit up with the tender, doe-eyed look of a mother. "I love her." She moved closer, stroking Casey's hair and lifting her small fingers. "My Lily will be two soon, and little West is five and a half months this week." Her eyes brightened. "We should get together sometimes. The kids should be friends. Maybe playmates one day."

Kara smiled. West had *two* children. It was hard to believe, and then it wasn't. He wasn't the same man she'd known three years ago. He was better. Happier. She glanced at Ryder, wanting more than anything to have a family with him one day. "I'd like that."

"Perfect." Tina clasped her hands to her chest, then grinned at Ryder as he moved toward the cabin door. "Hopefully we'll all be seeing a lot more of one another once this mess is resolved."

Ryder held the door and ushered the women inside. "I was surrounded by brothers for twenty-seven years, then I got hit with three sisters in the last eighteen months. And all of you are meddlesome."

Tina's smile widened. "So, that's a yes? We will be seeing more of you three, together, once this is over?"

Ryder rolled his eyes and went to pour coffee.

Kara blushed stupidly and took up a deep interest in Casey's hair. "Thank you for coming," she said.

"Did you have any trouble finding the place?" Ryder asked. "It's not easy for a reason."

Tina tipped her head left then right. "Not really. I made a couple of passes on the main road before I turned off. I wasn't sure there was really a road where I was told to turn. West had to draw me a map since it isn't on any."

Ryder set two mugs of coffee on the table, for Tina and Kara. "Was there anyone else on the road?"

"Was I followed?" Tina smiled. "I don't think so. I tried my best to be careful."

Ryder's expression hardened.

Tina either didn't notice, or she pretended not to.

Kara didn't like it. If Ryder was worried, she was downright terrified.

Tina twisted her mug on the wooden tabletop. "I could've called, but I'm not a fan of phones and texting is too impersonal for something so deeply personal. I wanted to give you my thoughts on Timothy

Sand, and be available when I finish in case you have any follow-up questions."

"All right." Ryder gripped the back of the empty chair beside Kara, unable or unwilling to sit still. He locked his elbows and leaned into the wood. "Hit me."

Tina moved her gaze from Ryder to Kara. "I've been reading up on arsonists this evening. I haven't worked with one in years, and I wanted to be sure I gave you the most accurate information I could. Forgive me if some of this is redundant. I'm sure you've done your own research." She released her mug in favor of folding her hands on the table in front of her. The sleeves of her tan cardigan matched beautifully with her cream tank top, khaki slacks and nude heels. She didn't look anything like a woman who'd marry the town sheriff, a man who preferred night fishing to restaurant dining, but this was clearly an example of opposites attracting each other. The most noticeable things about Tina were her warm smile and sincere blue eyes. Kara had known her for ten minutes and she already adored her. "You may know this, but there are six main reasons for a fire starting."

Ryder nodded.

"No," Kara said. "I don't."

"Vandalism." Tina lifted one manicured fingernail. "Excitement. Revenge." She raised another finger, then another, ticking off the reasons. "Crime concealment. Profit. And extremism." Her lips pressed into a firm line as she finished. "I think we can easily count out vandalism, profit and extremism."

Ryder crossed his arms and widened his stance, sliding effortlessly into marshal mode.

Kara worked to steady her breathing. Fear jumped all over her as she just thought of the man who'd led Ryder to the red sedan and tried to blow him up. Her hand went to his, needing to feel their connection.

Tina shifted in her seat. "I looked at all the case notes, the timelines and the revelations. Granted, I did it in a hurry because I think time is as valuable as accuracy at the moment, but there's a lot going on with this man."

"Like what?" Ryder asked, almost before she'd finished the statement. "Specifically."

"Well, for starters, I think the first fire he set was simply meant to be a crime concealment. He'd murdered his wife and her family, and he tried hastily to cover his tracks. He killed them first. Burned the house down afterward."

Kara looked to Ryder to see if he agreed.

He didn't speak, but he also didn't argue.

"The second fire," Tina said, "was revenge. Sand followed Jennifer Sayers home to punish her for aiding you to find him. He burned her home down for revenge."

"Different motives," Kara said, letting the criminal's variation in reasoning settle in. "Is that common?"

"No. But many pyromaniacs don't realize they are pyromaniacs until they're presented with the opportunity to set a fire and watch it consume something. I think the first fire was an act of desperation that happened to introduce him to his illness. Now he knows he likes fire, and the ones he's been setting in Shadow Point so far, bomb excluded of course, seem to be for the thrill of it. Sure, he's trying to get your attention—" she looked to Ryder "—but he could do that in lots of other ways. For example, I understand that he brought you here from another state just by having the right kind of conversation with the right person from your past. He's very clever."

"Manipulative," Ryder added with unnecessary snap. "Calculating."

"Yes," Tina agreed. "So, we know he doesn't need to start fires to get you to pay attention. He lights the fires because he likes it. Which moves him into the excitement category. The thrill and anticipation of striking the match is a strong motivation all by itself. Couple that with his desire for revenge against the marshal he blames for keeping him on the run, never letting him rest and possibly for forcing him to kill the Sayers family, and this is a recipe for disaster."

Shock and anger warred on Ryder's face. "You think he blames me for what he did to that family?"

"I think he can enjoy lighting the fires, but has incredible internal guilt over the murders. Especially the Sayers family because they weren't personal to him. Not like his wife and former in-laws."

"All of that is crazy," Ryder said. "He can't blame me for those murders."

"Because you already blame yourself?" Tina asked.

Ryder's face reddened. "I haven't chased him in a year. I'm not keeping him on the run." His words were clipped and impatient. "I wasn't even the marshal who arrested him or got him assigned to house arrest. I'm not in the picture," he barked. "Or I wasn't until he dragged me back here."

His words pierced Kara's heart. He made it sound as if he regretted returning here. She knew it wasn't what he'd meant, but it stung, nonetheless, especially after she'd let her hope rise and soar all day. Silly images of her with Casey and Ryder at the park, or in the backyard as a family, had wormed their way into her mind, as if they were possible, inevitable, guaranteed.

But nothing was guaranteed. Including her surviving this nightmare.

Tina watched Ryder carefully as he composed himself after nearly losing his temper. She took a tentative sip of her coffee, and pretended to smile at Casey, while letting her gaze slide sneakily back to Ryder several times. "I have a few more opinions," she said. "This is where my interpretation of the evidence gets dicey, and like I said, he's not my patient, so take this under consideration and nothing more."

"Go on," Ryder grouched.

"I think that in addition to his new thrill of setting fires and the pursuit of revenge against you, he's possibly dealing with a serious psychological issue."

Ryder made a deep, throaty noise. "No kidding."

"I've read his notebooks," Tina said. "He's definitely got something else going on as well. Possibly schizophrenia. Again, I'm only going on the information which was available to me, and I can't be sure without an interview of the patient, but the scribbles in his notebook suggest he may be hearing voices or that he believes he's following some kind of orders. It looks like he might have had a psychotic breakdown about six months ago when the note keeping began."

Ryder went still. His arms fell slack at his sides.

Kara raced backward through the loads of disturbing information she'd been given in the last few days, but she had no idea what Tina meant, or why Ryder had reacted that way. "What happened six months ago?" Kara asked, interrupting a stare-down between Tina and her brother-in-law.

Ryder lowered his eyes to Kara. "There was a vigil for Sand's ex-wife and her family around that time. The local church puts it on every year. It's nothing like the one for the Sayers. Not a rally or a call to action. Nothing like that. It's just a time of remembrance."

Tina formed a sad smile. "I think Sand wanted to attend, but couldn't because you were always there. You attended faithfully every year." She set her giant purse on the table and removed a folder from the contents. Tina opened the folder and selected a photo. "This is a copy of one of the pictures left at the hotel." She placed a fingertip beside Ryder's face among a two-dimensional crowd. Little red X's were scratched over his eyes. "It's a photo of the event covered by his hometown paper," she said. "You'd stopped hounding him, but you were still mucking up his life. The vigil is important to him. It's where it all started." She took another paper from her bag and turned it to face them. This was a newspaper clipping. "The morning after the vigil, Ryder was in the local paper for a commendation on a national case."

Kara lifted the newspaper clipping in awe. She'd had no idea how well Ryder had been doing. Come to think of it, he'd come back to her today instead of staying at the hotel room where Sand had vanished again. Pride lifted her chest. He really was better. Had his priorities right. Wanted her and Casey in his life. He hadn't acted like the obsessed man he'd once been during any part of this investigation, and the truth of it overtook her. Ryder was exactly who he said he was, a formerly broken man who had healed.

"I think Sand got some satisfaction while your life was spiraling," Tina said. "But watching your more recent successes go public when he couldn't even attend his wife's vigil without risk of capture and arrest, *by you*, might've pushed him over the edge."

Tina slid an apologetic look from Ryder to Kara. "I think that's why he targeted Kara. She was almost your wife once. That's close enough for him to make his point."

"Which is?" Ryder asked.

Tina eyeballed him. "How would you like to be kept from her?"

Ryder's hands landed protectively on Kara's shoulders as he moved behind her to stand. "That's not going to happen again."

Chapter Sixteen

Two long days dragged on with no visitors at the cabin, although Ryder's phone rarely stopped buzzing and dinging with texts and messages. Kara's nerves twisted into a fine point and jabbed at her heart and lungs. Her imagination grew darker and more detailed. Thoughts of a thousand ways Sand could appear and hurt them haunted her nights and days. Despite the busyness of Ryder's cell phone, it was always a new clue, but never a fresh sighting. Sand had turned to smoke.

For Kara, time alone with Casey and Ryder was both perfect and terrifying. Ryder left several times throughout the day, scouting the area, looking for signs a person had been in the woods nearby. His trips weren't long, but they left Kara on the brink of panic every time. What if Sand was out there and Ryder never came back? What if Sand was out there waiting to ambush her and Casey the moment they were alone?

Ryder took them on short hikes after dinner each night, never far from the cabin, but the change of scenery was always welcome. They walked a set of abandoned railroad tracks covered in leaves and forgotten by time. Ryder said the line had once been a direct route to Shadow Valley, a town now covered by water inside the national park, submerged long ago to manage flooding.

He'd led her through a pair of derelict passenger cars from the 1930s, dragging his hands over the dilapidated structures and telling her stories from his childhood. He and his brothers had staged elaborate games of cops and robbers, using the cars as hideouts, shelters and occasionally army barracks.

The cars had given Kara the chills, sitting at odd angles, the tracks beneath them half-sunken in the earth. Their once-shiny metal walls were scored with mud, their floors drowned in leaves. The wide viewing windows were empty, the glass long gone. Kara could almost see the ghosts of past travelers seated on the faded and cracked vinyl seats or standing single file down the center, awaiting a stop that would never come.

Ryder had smiled as they passed the cars on their way back to the cabin, but Kara was glad to put them behind her.

At night, she curled on the couch beside him.

"Any news?" she asked, leaning her head against his strong arm.

"No." Ryder's frame was tense.

She felt the muscle of his biceps clench beneath

her ear as he answered. "No?" Kara straightened and twisted for a better look at his face.

His gaze jumped from window to window as it did most nights when the forest grew inconceivably still. "I don't know what he's waiting for. Where he is. I keep thinking something big is coming. This quiet can't last."

"Can't it?" she asked. "Can't he have given up and left town?" Kara's heart pleaded for it to be true. "He avoided his wife's vigil every year because he didn't want to risk going to jail. And he must know he can't accomplish whatever it is he wanted to do with a dozen lawmen looking for him around the clock. His face is plastered on every news spot in the county." She raised her brows. "Maybe he gave up. Went home."

"Maybe." Ryder wrapped a protective arm over her shoulders and settled her back against his side, tucking her in close and holding her tight.

It was impossible not to hear the "No" in his answer.

"What's the latest news, then?" she pushed. Something had him on edge all day, and he hadn't come out with it on his own. She was tired of waiting. "What does West say? Or Blake?"

Ryder released a long, tired breath. "West thinks it's not too late to put you and Casey on a plane to Timbuktu while I go after Sand full force until he's locked up somewhere he can't ever hurt you."

"And Blake?" Kara asked. Ryder likely got feedback, requested and otherwise, from everyone out there looking for Sand, but the feedback that mattered most would come from his brothers.

"Blake thinks we should stay at his place, and keep a SWAT team on standby until Sand loses his patience and makes a move."

Kara hated both options for different reasons, but living on a mountain was going to be a problem when winter came, or Casey started school in five years. "What do you think?"

"I'm leaning toward Timbuktu," Ryder said with another deep exhale. "We've been in this strange stalemate too long, and I don't like it. I'm going to have to do something to put things in motion again, but my first priority is keeping you and Casey safe."

"Okay." Kara ran a palm over his arm.

"Okay?" he parroted, a note of surprise in his voice. "Timbuktu? Just like that?"

"I mean, I'd rather go to Paris, but I trust your judgement." She traced the dips and grooves of his torso with one finger. Counting abs. Admiring pecs. "I just got you back. It's hard to think of leaving. But it's even harder to think of Sand getting his hands on Casey." An involuntary shiver rocked down her spine. "That's…not something I can live with."

Ryder trapped her roaming hand in his and twined their fingers. "You don't have to go to Timbuktu. If you're willing, I can ask the marshal's service to treat you like a witness until this is over." He dropped their joined hands against his thigh. "I should've looked into that immediately."

"Hey." She turned her face up to his. "We're okay. You've kept us safe, and if you want us to go, we'll go. We trust you to protect us. Whatever comes."

"Tomorrow," he said. "We'll move you both off the mountain after breakfast, so I can get back out there and help end this. I put in the paperwork for your temporary relocation this afternoon. I didn't know how to tell you."

Kara could hear sacrifice in his words. She could feel it in his touch. Ryder wanted to be her sole protector, but he also needed to hunt this monster. He couldn't do both.

He repositioned his arms around her, tipping her back and lowering her onto the couch. He covered her body with his, slowly, intentionally. Ryder was saying goodbye.

"Will you come for us after you catch him? Bring us back to you." A renegade tear slid from the corner of her eye and over her temple. Kara had no doubt that the marshals would keep her and Casey safe. She worried about what would happen to Ryder. "You have to be careful, too. You're not invincible, and Sand is crazy."

He kissed her eyelids, pulling back after each gentle press of his lips, as if he was memorizing the details of her face. "I promise."

A knot of emotion tightened in her throat. "Is this what you were thinking about all day? Sending me away?" He'd been quieter than normal, distant. She'd thought for sure he'd been withholding bad news. That maybe Sand had hurt someone else in the name of hurting Ryder. She'd never expected that he'd been worried about asking her to go with the marshals. She knew he wouldn't ask unless it was for the best.

He pinned her with sincere blue eyes. "No. I've been thinking of how I might convince you to stay with me when this is over."

A small smile budded on her lips. "You weren't trying to figure out a way to deliver bad news or ask me to leave without upsetting me?"

Ryder bunched his brows together. "Not unless wanting to make you mine, officially, upsets you." He leaned on one elbow and stroked the spot on her finger where his engagement ring had once lived.

A ragged gasp tore from her lips. Her thumb still went to that spot sometimes, wishing things had been different.

"I know it's only been a few days since I showed up without an invitation, and hauling the absolute worst kind of trouble. I put you in danger. Put Casey in danger."

"You've been thinking about marriage?" The words were soft on her tongue, floating away from her in small whispers.

For a moment, his expression fell.

Was she wrong? Had she made an obnoxious, embarrassing leap? He'd only touched her ring finger, and she'd blurted the word *marriage*. Heat rolled over her cheeks. "Sorry. I didn't mean to assume. You touched my finger, and I am so stupid." She raised a hand to shield her humiliated face. "Can we pretend I didn't say that?"

Ryder sniffed hard. Emotion glossed his eyes. "You aren't wrong."

She straightened with a snap. "What?"

He smiled. "But that has to wait."

"For what?" She knew the answer. *Sand.* Everything had suddenly become all about Sand.

"Hey." Ryder kissed her hand and slid onto his knees in front of the couch. "You deserve a proposal without *him* looming in the background."

Kara scooted to the edge of the couch and locked her wrists around his neck, her ankles around his back. "I would marry you anytime. Anywhere. And no one could ever put a smudge on that." She kissed his square jawline. His sexy dimpled chin. "Sand came here to take me away from you, but he's brought you back to me instead. And I'm never letting go."

Ryder's lids drooped. His gaze fell to her lips.

Kara's insides heated and flipped. "If I'm leaving in the morning, you might want to send me off properly."

Ryder pulled her off the couch and flipped her onto the floor with ease. "Tomorrow, I'm getting you away from here, and I'm going to overturn every stone in Cade County until I find Timothy Sand. When I'm done, I'm going to beg you to marry me."

Kara pulled his face down to hers. "And what about right now?"

Ryder planted a slow, bone-melting kiss on her lips, then let his hands and mouth wander. Her heart pounded recklessly from the effects of his skilled touch. Her mind was limp with endorphins and bliss before he paused to check on her well-being. "You okay?" he asked with a proud grin.

She nodded, breathless. "Take off your clothes."

Ryder's eyes darkened. "You first."

COOL AIR SWEPT over Kara's chest. She reached for Ryder on the floor beside her, but he was gone. The slow glow of daybreak flickered on the horizon outside the cabin's living room window.

"Ryder?" she asked softly, rising onto her elbows and pulling on her discarded shirt.

The room around her was still. Only the sound of Casey's steady breathing carried to Kara's ears through the baby monitor at her side.

She wiped the sleep from her eyes and finished dressing.

It wasn't unusual for Ryder to slip away and check on things. It was odd, though, that he hadn't woken her to watch the sunrise. She'd enjoyed those precious moments yesterday with him at her side.

Kara cleaned up the pillows and blankets tossed haphazardly on the floor.

Ryder's clothes were gone. She could discount a trip to the bathroom. He must've gone outside.

She inched toward the front window, wondering what time it was and how long she'd been asleep. She didn't feel rested. Granted, she'd enjoyed quite a workout before nodding off.

Beyond the glass, the haze of dawn hovered strangely in the air. Normally, the fog hung like clouds in the trees where the cabin's yard turned to cliffs, and clung to the ground near the porch, but it was different this morning.

An unpleasant scent set her intuition on edge. She knew in the next heartbeat that the smell filtering beneath the door, stinging her nose and scratching her throat, was smoke.

Fear shot through her as she turned for another look outside. It wasn't dawn. Wasn't fog. There was a fire burning on the horizon and the smoke was crawling its way into the cabin.

Kara grabbed her phone and dialed Ryder.

The line connected instantly, but he didn't bother with formalities. "I'm right out front."

She darted into the night to wait for him.

A moment later, his silhouette emerged from the thin gray smoke. "He found us."

Kara covered her face with both hands, begging herself not to scream. There would be time for screaming later. Right now, they needed to get out of there. "Can we make it off the mountain?" She nodded to Mr. Garrett's truck.

Or were the fires burning across the only access road they had?

"We're going to try," Ryder said. "I walked as far as I could to get an idea of where the fire originated, but I can't tell. Smoke's too thick. I had to turn back. Good news is the flames are still far away, and I've got an army headed in our direction. The fire department will take care of the fire, rescue teams will meet us en route off this mountain."

A tiny bubble of relief rose in her chest. The fire wasn't close yet, and help was on the way. "Do we have enough volunteer firefighters to handle this? It seems really big, and the drought…"

Ryder didn't bother looking at the orange glow burning through the smoke. "West's already spoken with every volunteer in four counties. It'll take some men longer than others to get here, but they're coming, and we're going to need all the hands we can get. If we're lucky, the winds won't change and take the fire into town."

Kara forced images of burning homes from her mind. "I'll get Casey."

Ryder nodded. "I'm going to keep walking the perimeter. Just in case."

Air pressed from her lungs as she interpreted the thing he didn't say. *In case Sand is already here.*

Kara hurried to the room where Casey slept. The moan of the swinging front door stopped her short of lifting her baby into her arms. She froze, arms extended, body tipped forward, waiting.

The sound of creaking floorboards followed. Someone was in the front room, and it wasn't Ryder. He would've called out to her or been at her side by now.

"Knock, knock," a hoarse voice echoed through the cabin. "Anyone home?"

Kara scooped Casey into her arms and grabbed an extra blanket. She snuggled her baby tight and bounced her gently in an effort to keep her asleep. She knew that voice too well.

Sand.

She sent up a silent prayer that he'd sneaked past Ryder, and that Ryder was unharmed out there in the smoke and growing forest fire.

She unscrewed the lid from her water bottle left beside the rocking chair and dumped it over the spare baby blanket, saturating as much of the thin material as possible.

"Dear," the voice rasped, "it seems you are home after all. Taking a bath?" he asked.

Kara stopped, her eyes darting over the room, as if he might actually be present with her somehow.

The baby monitor glowed beside the playpen.

Her stomach dropped, and her pulse raced. *Be calm. Be calm. Think*, she begged herself.

The curtain billowed beside an open window, and Kara tiptoed closer to push the screen wide. She kissed Casey's head, then climbed onto the narrow ledge, baby fussing quietly in her arms.

She let the curtain fall behind her, then jumped

lithely onto her feet in the forest behind the cabin. A small, two- or three-foot drop, but it had felt like multiple stories. Casey's eyes blinked and rolled, trying to wake, but not yet ready.

"Shh." Kara arranged the dampened blanket like a shield covering Casey's head and shoulders against the growing cloud of smoke.

The ominous orange glow had risen higher in the sky, illuminating the mountain in eerie shades of red and casting shadows over the little cabin.

"Ah, ah, ah," the voice sounded at her ear. The man from the park, *Timothy Sand*, stood behind her, inside the bedroom window where she'd been just seconds before.

"Ryder!" Kara screamed and leapt away from the cabin. "Ryder!"

She ran until her sides began to ache from the smoke inhalation. Her ankle turned, and she stumbled over the edge of the mountain, barely staying upright with the help of a nearby tree. She looked for Ryder in the thickening cloud, but there was no one and nothing. Even Sand had vanished from view.

Casey whined, all but forgotten in her mother's trembling arms.

"Shh," she cooed, watching the baby's heavy lids attempt to pull open. Her button nose wrinkled and her tiny mouth pulled down into a deep frown. "No-nono. Shh. Shh. Shh." Kara turned in a frantic circle, squinting against the thickening smoke that stung her eyes and muddied up the already dark forest around her. Even the moon couldn't be seen through the suffocating, acrid air.

"Kara!" Ryder's angry voice echoed through the hills.

She spun in search of him, babying her tender ankle.

A twig snapped nearby, and Kara began to run again, no longer sure which way the cabin had been, only that it was up the hill, and she was fumbling quickly down it, toward the river that would lead her to town. Panic clutched her like a vise, insisting she stop moving, stay, hide, but she had a plan, and she was sticking to it, twisted ankle, burning throat and all. Another few yards and the air began to clear. She sipped thirstily at the untainted oxygen, clearing her lungs and attempting to unscramble her thoughts.

Her ringing cell phone nearly sent her out of her skin, and she groped for it in her pocket. "Ryder?" His face lit her screen.

"Where are you? Are you okay?" he asked, racing through the words.

"I'm down the mountain," she said. A cough ripped through her words. "He's here." She stopped again, unable to continue speaking. The winds shifted, pushing a wall of smoke in her direction and bringing the licking flames into view. The fire crawled branch to branch high overhead, it rode on embers through the air, and it landed in a blanket of dried and fallen leaves at her feet, igniting small flames. Her head grew fuzzy as she stomped the leaves. Her face grew slick with sweat.

"Where's Casey?" Ryder asked, a mix of fear and hope in his voice.

"With me." She coughed. "I can't breathe." She turned away from the reaching inferno, unsteady on her feet. One ankle throbbing. Her chest, eyes, nose and throat aching.

"I'm coming," Ryder vowed. "West and the others are almost here. Firefighters are in place. Sit down. Get your head below the smoke and let me come to you," he instructed. "I will find you."

"Okay."

"Tell me what you can see," he said.

A rough hand landed on her shoulder, gripping her tight, aggressive and unforgiving. The sting of serrated metal cut through her tender flesh at her throat. "Hello, Mrs. Garrett," Timothy Sand whispered into her ear. His body pressed against her back. "You're a hard woman to catch up with."

"Kara?" Ryder asked. "Kara?" He barked her name, and it echoed through the hot and glowing world around her.

Her phone fell into the leaves at her feet as Sand dug his fingers into her hair and yanked her down the mountain.

Chapter Seventeen

Kara whimpered, fighting screams of pain as Timothy Sand dragged her over the smoky hillside. Her scalp burned and ached as more strands ripped free in his relentless grip.

Casey cried in her arms, but Kara couldn't find focus beyond the pain to coo or comfort her. The best she could offer was not to scream while holding Casey tightly to her chest.

Screaming would only make Kara cough again, make her dizzy again. And she suspected Sand wouldn't have a problem shoving the blade he held at her throat as deep as necessary if she gave him a reason. So she stayed as quiet as possible, trying not to frighten Casey or make her baby cry any louder. She could picture her tiny infant lungs filling with the ghastly smoke already.

Instead, Kara dragged her twisted foot against the ground behind them, leaving a trail, she hoped, like Hansel and Gretel, for her hero to find.

The path would have been obvious in normal conditions, but the fast-moving fire and wall of darkening smoke made it hard for her to see. Hopefully Ryder wouldn't miss it.

Scarlet and amber flames licked the night sky above the smoke, changing the beautiful summer forest into the wicked, twisted setting of a Grimm's fairy tale.

Kara clung to the hope that none of this would stop Ryder. He was raised in these woods, trained to track and hunt. He would find her as long as she kept dragging that foot.

Sand stopped abruptly and the knife dug deeper into the tender flesh of her throat. "Here," he said, swinging her around to face the other direction.

The decrepit passenger cars came into view. "No," she gasped. *Anywhere but there. Anywhere but the abandoned tombs of a forgotten train.* Despite the growing fires, a ghastly chill overcame her as Sand shoved her inside.

Kara stumbled on her useless ankle, nearly dropping her infant as she tumbled painfully onto the first seat.

Sand loomed over her, glaring down with soot-stained cheeks and bits of ash clinging in his hair. "Put her down."

Kara gripped Casey tighter, her impending death registering like a hard slap to the face. "No."

He ground his teeth and leaned in close, positioning the tip of his broad hunting knife against her temple. His hot stinky breath washed over her face. "Then I'll kill you now and take her with me."

Kara bit back a thousand venomous retorts. There was no way she was letting him take her baby. "Okay," she agreed. "Put your knife away." She waited while he lowered the blade, then she laid Casey on the seat beside her.

"Good girl." Sand shoved the knife into the holster on his belt and moved behind Kara. "Now, give me your hands."

She pulled them back. "Why?" Her stomach lurched and churned as she awaited the answer. Would he cut her again? Burn her? Tie her up? The last possibility scared her most. How could she escape with her hands tied behind her back? She couldn't carry Casey, and she wouldn't leave without her. She batted stinging eyes and searched the dense smoke outside the missing windows. *Ryder, where are you?*

Sand snarled. He grabbed her, apparently done waiting for her compliance, and twisted her arms roughly toward him. He tied her wrists to the rusted metal rod along the seatback, dragging her hands carelessly across the sharp and broken edges. "You were supposed to be married," he complained. "It's not the same if you aren't married."

She didn't have to ask what that meant. Tina had speculated that the final straw for Sand was probably the fact that Ryder kept him from his dead wife's vigil. A woman who was dead because *he* killed her.

"Then let us go," Kara begged. A new idea forming. "I'm not his wife. She's not his baby." The words sent a spear of raw pain through her gut. Kara wanted a future with Ryder, but more than that, she wanted Casey to have a future. "Let us go and find whatever woman he loves in Ohio. He moved there when he left here three years ago, and he didn't come back until you showed up. He's not here for me," she cried. "He's here for you."

Sand moved back in front of her where she could see him, a look of amusement on his face. "He may have come for me, but he got you first." His sick, demented face turned red with delight. "A few hours ago. On the cabin floor, I believe."

Bile flooded Kara's mouth.

Sand had been outside the cabin while she and Ryder made love. "You were watching." Her skin crawled and she fought the urge to puke. How long had he known they were there? How long had they thought they were safe, but it was just more of his game?

"It was hard not to watch," he said. "Impossible to deny your love." He turned the corners of his mouth in disgust. "I could sit back and wait for you to marry, but I think ruining things for him a second time seems the stronger move."

"How did you find us?" Kara asked, biding her time and praying for just a little more.

Keep him talking, she thought. *Ryder is looking for us. A rescue team is coming.*

Just. Don't. Die.

Sand sucked his teeth and frowned impossibly deeper. "I was worried I wouldn't find you when you left town after the car bomb, but I wasn't in a hurry. Nowhere to go, you know?" He dug into one of the pockets of his camouflaged cargo pants and liberated a squeeze bottle of lighter fluid. "I went back to the sheriff's department after things settled down at my hotel room. Had to borrow a new car." He shrugged. "I saw a fancy lady talking with the sheriff about me. He had photos of me and a pile of papers. He gave it all to her. I thought she was a reporter or a fed." He twisted the bottle's little red cone cap with his teeth, then spit it onto the floor. "He walked her to her car after that, and he kissed her right on the mouth."

Tina.

"She had her hands on his chest—" Sand put a hand over his heart "—like this, and there it was. A wedding ring." He turned the lighter fluid over and sprayed it up Kara's legs, then squeezed a line of it on her lap and over her torso.

She braced herself, fighting the urge to scream. Casey's cries were already moving from general complaint to serious demand, and she didn't want to make them worse. Kara wiggled away from her baby, pressing herself against the mud-streaked wall and putting as much space as possible between her lighter-fluid-soaked clothing and Casey. With any luck, the flames wouldn't jump to her when Sand struck the match.

She promised herself not to scream when it happened. She didn't want Casey to hear it, and somehow recall the dying screams of her mother being burned alive.

The empty bottle made an ugly gurgle, and he tossed it aside, pulling another from his pocket. "That's when it hit me," he said. "If I couldn't find one Garrett's wife, I'd just use another one to get to the first. So, I followed Mrs. Sheriff home. Or, I thought I did." Sand cast his gaze into the blowing gray smoke beyond the train car.

The wind had changed direction, putting them in the path of destruction.

Kara coughed against the onslaught of smoke.

Sand's eyes were distant, unmoved by the fast-moving wall of fire in the distance. He was somewhere else. Not with her inside the dilapidated train car, on a mountaintop he'd set on fire.

"You followed her here," Kara guessed, choking on the acrid air. *Keep him talking. If he's talking, then he isn't killing you or touching Casey.*

He dragged his attention back to her. "When she turned her fancy car into the trees, I thought she was crazy." He shook his head, then seemed to recall his mission to burn down Kentucky. He went back to spraying the pungent liquid over every seat along the aisle. "I parked my car and followed her. It was easy. I walked alongside her, slipping between the trees right to your door."

Kara tugged and twisted her arms behind her, testing the strength of her bindings. The material was rough and narrow like twine, but wrapped several times around each wrist, making it impossible to break. She pulled the binding tight between her wrists, separating her hands as much as possible to protect them, then she dragged the twine across the edges of jagged metal, attempting to saw herself free. The ragged edge of rusted metal cut into her skin as she worked, drenching her palms in hot, sticky blood.

Sweat rolled over her forehead and dripped into her eyes as the fire drew near and the temperature rose dramatically around her.

Casey thrashed and kicked at her blankets, demanding to be held, and desperately needing water and fresh air.

Sand continued to pull little bottles from his giant cargo pockets and cover everything in sight with lighter fluid. He moved backward through the open door, doodling destruction and dropping the empty bottles in his wake. With two fresh bottles, he stepped outside, spraying the door and ground before moving out of sight.

Breath caught in Kara's throat. He'd left her there for a reason. Next would be the match. She imagined the flames erupting, circling the car, sealing her fate. All while she couldn't even hold her baby to say goodbye.

As if Casey could feel Kara's desperation, her cries grew relentlessly fevered.

"Shut her up!" Sand called through the open door,

having made a full circle around the car. His eyes were wild, his expression feral as he emptied the final containers. He jerked his head left, then right, turning side to side in search of something. "Shut up!"

All Kara heard was the cry of her terrified infant and the growing roar of a fire chewing through the forest to meet them. She recalled the soaring embers, landing in leaves and igniting the forest floor. She didn't want to think about what one floating ember could do to the train car, or to her.

Sand pressed his palms against his ears.

Kara worked more doggedly at the twine between her wrists.

"Shut. Her. Up!" Sand screamed, his face morphing into something animalistic in the haze of smoke. "Do it now, or I will." His hunting knife was back in hand.

"Shh," Kara cooed, but the efforts were swallowed by Casey's desperation. "I need to hold her," Kara said. "She's too upset. She won't calm down on her own now." Kara had only let Casey get this upset once before. She was three days old, and Kara could barely move following her C-section. The healing had been harder and slower than the nurses at the hospital had promised, and the extra-strength pain killers weren't doing much to help her manage the pain. She was exhausted, hurting, depressed and alone. And Kara had let Casey cry while she sobbed along with her in her own bed, too unsteady to trust her legs to carry her to the nursery. She'd fallen asleep despite her infant's wails, and she'd woken feeling like another woman, but she'd vowed never to put Casey through that again. Every day since then, she'd paid close attention to her baby's needs and met them, often before Casey had thought to complain. "I have to hold her," she repeated, louder this time. "She needs to know I'm still here."

Sand's face was red, his hands smashed tight to his ears.

Kara tipped her face nearer Casey's ear. "You are my sunshine," she sang in a raspy, quavering voice, trying to draw her baby's attention, but it was too late. Casey was in a spiral, and she wouldn't recover without her touch.

If her hands were free, Kara could hold her. If her hands were free, she had a chance of escaping with Casey.

She had to get them out of there before Sand struck a match.

Casey's cries grew strange and labored. Her face turned frighteningly red with heat and frustration. Her fingers were curled into little fists in the air. It seemed impossible that she could withstand the smoke much longer without the worst kind of consequences.

"Please," Kara begged.

Sand stalked forward, up the angled step and into the train car with menace on his brow. He unleashed a rectangular silver lighter from his pocket and opened the lid with the flick of one thumb.

"Stop," Kara begged. "Don't do this. You don't have to do this."

"I do," he said, eyes locked on her screaming baby. "I really, really do."

Kara threw herself over Casey, shielding her despite her lighter fluid-soaked clothes. Anything was better than letting Sand get his hands on her. "No." She tightened her jaw and dragged her bindings over the jagged metal once more, lining the thinnest section of material against the sharpest point of the bar. She leaned her weight into the efforts, desperate to finish the job. "You will not touch my baby."

Sand barked a laugh. He flicked the lighter shut then open, his thumb petting the tiny wheel that would call a flame to life at his command. "I'm trying to decide if Marshal Garrett would be more upset knowing the baby watched you die, or if it would be worse for him to know you watched her die. Before you die. So, who. Goes. First?"

He flipped the lid back and forth a few more times, rubbing the little gear with his thumb, never letting the fire erupt.

"He's going to kill you for this," Kara seethed, not caring if it was completely true, only that Sand knew he would pay soundly for whatever he did next.

"I think I'll start with the baby," he decided.

Kara curled her fists into tight knots.

Sand stepped closer. "Get out of the way." He grabbed Kara's hip and tried to swing her away from Casey, but Kara fought.

She kicked him in the knees and shins, still hung up by her bound wrists and one narrowing portion of twine.

He stumbled back with a roar, grabbing his knee-cap and snarling. "You bitch!" He bared his teeth and raised his hands, coming at her as if he planned to strangle her.

But Kara had had enough.

She set her jaw, planted her feet against the floor of the forsaken passenger car and lunged at him. The remaining threads of twine sliced through her already bleeding skin and ripped her left thumb out of its socket.

The force of her momentum snapped the final binding and set her free.

His eyes went wide with shock as she collided with him, knocking him through the door backward and rolling them both against the water-starved earth, soaked in lighter fluid.

Kara screamed as her ankle gave a deafening crack.

Sand rolled her off him and reclaimed his fallen lighter. He held it toward the train car where Casey still screamed in terror, desperate for her mother, for help, anything but the thick gray smoke swallowing the train car and the lunatic wielding a lighter outside.

"No!" Kara slapped his arm, unable to reach the lighter as intended.

The resounding strike of his hand against her cheek sent stars through her vision. Her ears began to ring. Her back hit the earth with a thud, expelling the air from her lungs in one fell whoosh. She blinked her way back from a near blackout, pressing one palm to her scorching cheek, and forcing herself onto her knees. "Please!" she cried. "Don't hurt my baby."

Sand's expression went flat. His body motionless. He slid wild eyes toward the suddenly silent train car.

Kara listened harder. The unstoppable soul-twisting wails of her infant had stopped. Smoke filled the car until there seemed to be no car at all. There was only fire, smoke and Sand.

"No!" She lurched forward and vomited.

The soft snick of the lighter in his hand turned her crying eyes upward. The flame danced, reflected in Sand's dark eyes. "Say goodbye, Mommy."

Behind him Ryder's silhouette moved into view, cutting a path through the suffocating smoke. Kara blinked through the haze.

Ryder raised his gun in unison with Sand's lighter. Before Sand could toss the flame that would engulf the train car and steal her daughter's precious life,

Ryder brought him down with the butt of his gun. Sand collapsed like a ragdoll at Kara's feet.

The lighter and its deadly flame fell in slow motion toward the lighter-fluid-saturated leaves.

Chapter Eighteen

A wall of flames shot into existence, climbing the treetops and enveloping the train car.

"Casey!" Kara's clothes were alight with fire, flames racing over the lines of fluid Sand had sprayed on her and eating up the twigs and leaves along the ground.

For a moment, the sudden wave of heat stole her breath. Then, the excruciating pain took over, sending a long piercing scream from her core.

Ryder dove through the smoke and flames. A crushing blow smashed the air from her lungs as he covered her body with his and sent them into a united spiral over the hillside. He clung impossibly tighter to her with every beat of unforgiving earth.

They rolled to a stop several yards away, landing in a spot with clearer air and flameless leaves. The fire on her clothes had gone out, but the pain remained. On her skin. In her heart.

"Casey!" Kara bawled. She'd survived being set on fire, survived the serial arsonist's capture, and if there were miracles like those available for her today, then there had to be one more for Casey. Kara's aching mother's heart wouldn't survive the alternative. "Casey!" She pushed onto her feet as Ryder rolled off her. Another scream tore from her throat. "My ankle," she croaked, then attempted to hobble toward her daughter.

Ryder wound strong arms around her back and hoisted her upright. "Your wrists and throat are cut. You're bleeding. Covered in burns." He scooped her feet off the ground. His eyes were wild with fear and worry. "Uncle Henry's at the cabin. Tell me all your injuries. How long have you been bleeding?"

"Stop." Kara struggled against his iron grip, but he locked her in tight. "Go back to the train," she cried. "Get Casey! She stopped crying. I think she's…" Fat tears of fear and grief stole Kara's words. Her arms reached uselessly toward the passenger car now completely concealed in flame.

Ryder carried her away, giving the site a wide berth.

"Casey's fine. You're not. Stop fighting."

"No," she sobbed, unable to make sense of his words. "My baby." Kara clamped shaking hands over her mouth as he continued to move away from Casey. Blood smeared across her lips and chin. Why wouldn't he listen? Maybe he didn't know? "She was in the train car." Kara's words fell like stones from her lips. Heavy. Impossible.

"She's okay," Ryder said again. "Control your breaths. The smoke gets thicker up here."

Kara tried to obey. Tried to think beyond the fear.

The fire seemed to have retreated, leaving a path of charred wilderness in its wake.

Somehow, the forest had burst into a flurry of activity. Firefighters, lawmen, strangers in oxygen masks and coveralls had appeared everywhere. Where was her baby? How could she possibly have survived this? Outside the now-smoldering train car, two men in US Marshals jackets stood over a lifeless figure, doused in the white chemicals of a fire extinguisher.

"They don't have her," Kara demanded, punching Ryder's shoulder and thrusting against his chest. "Go back!"

Casey's sharp cry broke through the air, and Kara froze.

The sound came again, not from the abandoned car, but from far away, maybe as high up the mountain as the cabin. "Casey?" she whispered, daring to dream.

She turned her face in search of the sound. "I don't understand," she choked out, coughing roughly and fighting another wave of nausea.

"She's fine," he promised. "At the ambulance with Cole and Uncle Henry."

"How?"

"Cole stole her through the open window of the train car, after you lobbed yourself at a killer."

Kara's heart lifted and fresh tears sprung to her eyes. "What?"

"I had Sand in my sights. It would have been a clean shot until you knocked him on his ass and went tumbling through the train car door."

"You saw that?" she asked, her ears still tuned closely to the beloved screams of her baby.

"Everyone saw that." He swept his gaze through the space around them. "I told you West and his deputies were already on their way and the fire trucks were dispatched. My team, Blake and his men, were all en route. I met them at the crest of the hill while you went for Casey, but when I went for you, you were gone."

"He was in the cabin," she said, the awful memory of him in the bedroom window behind her flashing back to mind.

"Lucky for me you're smart. You left the world's most obvious trail behind you."

"I thought you wouldn't be able to find it in the smoke. I thought you wouldn't come."

"Baby," he said, slowing to look into her eyes, "I will always come for you."

Kara kissed Ryder's cheek. She pulled herself closer to him and held on tight, the burn of her thighs and stomach returning with each jostle and jolt as he climbed the hillside with her in his arms.

Back on the mountaintop, the red lights of emergency vehicles swam over the charred remains of the Garrett family cabin. Firefighters on four-wheelers, carrying backpacks of water, worked to squelch the glowing embers that threatened to start the flames all over again.

Many of the firefighters wore different-colored uniforms emblazoned with a half-dozen town names. West really had rallied men and women from all over.

But the best sight of all was her baby.

Cole stood awkwardly, bobbing a screaming Casey beside Uncle Henry's ambulance. She'd been cleaned up and wrapped in a white hospital-issue blanket. Uncle Henry pressed a stethoscope to her heart while she wailed.

Cole's head jerked up suddenly, eyes locked on Ryder as he crossed the final few yards to Cole's side. "You're both okay?" Cole asked. He looked them over with a mix of awe and joy.

"No," Ryder rasped, letting loose on a smoke-induced cough. "She's hurt her ankle, her wrists and throat are bleeding, and the sonofabitch set her on fire."

Uncle Henry swung the ambulance doors wide, his eyes stretching with shock. "Heavens. Put her down in the bus." He watched Kara carefully. "Your baby is just fine. Dehydrated and pissed off, but she's going to be all right. We've given her oxygen and cleaned her up nicely." He checked her wrist and neck wounds as he spoke, following her into the ambulance, stethoscope already pressed to her chest.

Kara stiffened as Ryder climbed back outside. "Don't leave."

He collected Casey from Cole, then returned with a fierce expression on his brow. "Never."

Uncle Henry started an IV line.

Cole shut the ambulance doors and gave them a pat.

The ambulance rumbled to life, and Kara's world grew hazy.

Ryder spoke softly to Casey, kissing her hands and face.

Kara imagined the glimmer of a tear on his cheek as her eyes pulled shut with fatigue and possibly the effects of whatever was in that IV bag.

FALL LEAVES FLUTTERED to the ground at Kara's feet, thrown from the gorgeous gold-and-scarlet covered trees. Trick-or-treat night had always been her favorite as a child, and though it had previously lost a little interest for her as an adult, seeing Casey bundled in her puffy white marshmallow costume had put trick-or-treat back at the top of Kara's list.

Ryder pointed his camera at them again. "Get her belly," he said, a big smile on his face. "That always cracks her up."

Kara poked the puffy costume at its center. "I can't get anywhere near her belly. You're going to have to make do with that look of general glee she has going."

"Fine." He lowered the camera and exchanged it for Casey, pulling the nearly eight-month-old baby to his face for a snuggle. "Who's the most beautiful princess in the world?"

Kara snapped a photo, capturing another of her favorite moments forever. Her heart warmed at the sight of them together.

"What?" he asked, tucking Casey back into her stroller.

"Nothing."

Ryder rounded the front of the stroller and ran his palms over Kara's hips before catching her in the curves of her waist.

"I'm just really happy," she said. "Happy you're home. Happy to be alive." Happy her burns had all healed with minimal scarring, and that the snap of her ankle had only been a fracture, not something that had required surgery. Most of all, she was happy her baby girl had no lasting effects from that horrible night in the burning forest.

The Garretts had lost their cabin, a piece of their history, to Timothy Sand, but they'd all assured her countless times that they much preferred the things they got to keep. Everyone they loved had made it out alive, and Ryder had proposed before she'd even left the hospital. Then, he did it again at his parents' house where everyone could see. Apparently, his brothers had started a new tradition in his family. If the whole clan wasn't present, it didn't happen.

Ryder kissed her cheek. "I love you," he said, in the same tone of awe he seemed to use since she'd said yes from her hospital bed. He raised her hand in his, heavy with the most beautiful ring she'd ever seen, and he kissed the puckered skin along her wrist. Ironically, she'd done more damage to herself, attempting to free her hands from Sand's twine than he had by dousing her in lighter fluid. The burns on her legs and torso were all but invisible, even to her knowing eyes, but the scars at her wrists would forever remind her of just how strong and resilient her new family really was.

"I love you, too." Her skin warmed with the truth of it.

Sand had done his best to take everything from Kara, but he'd actually given her more than she thought was possible. Until he'd shown up at the park, Kara had thought a life alone with Casey was all she needed. She hadn't dared to dream of what her days could be with Ryder back at her side. For that, she was almost thankful the fugitive had returned. She only hated that Sand hadn't lived to see their engagement announced in the paper. He hadn't survived the burns and smoke inhalation he'd suffered after dropping his lighter and igniting the circle around the train car where he'd fallen.

"We're going to be late again," she whispered. A bad habit she and Ryder had developed since he'd moved back in. It was hard to get anywhere on time when she couldn't keep her hands off him. With that thought, she turned her lips to his ear. "Maybe after the Halloween party we can go home and celebrate some more."

He rolled his forehead against hers and gave a deep throaty moan. "You're making it hard for me not to turn around right now."

Kara smiled. "We've got an announcement to make. Remember? Everyone has to hear about our little day trip today, or it didn't happen."

Ryder's smile broadened. He straightened to his full height and looked down at her with deep pride in his eyes, hands clutching the thick, goofy costume material at her sides. "When we get home, I'm peeling this big candy wrapper off of you nice and slow."

"Why?" she teased, striking a pose in her giant chocolate bar costume. "I say we leave it on."

Ryder barked a belly laugh, and Casey joined in from her seat in the stroller, clapping her dimpled hands and laughing, gleeful at the sound of his joy.

Kara took position at the stroller's helm and began to move toward Blake and Marissa's house a few blocks away. Ryder looked positively good enough to eat in his big ole graham cracker costume, and she wasn't kidding about that private after-party.

He kept pace with her, one arm around her back, waving at their neighbors, passing treats out to tiny knights, pirates and cheerleaders. "I'm seeing a lot of dressed-up folks tonight, but I dare someone to say my family isn't the best-looking s'mores ingredients they've ever seen."

Kara leaned against him, letting his perfect words sink in, her heart swelling impossibly further. She and Casey and Ryder were a family.

Other couples and hordes of kids streamed around them on the leaf-speckled streets illuminated by lamplights and echoing with peals of laughter.

"I think this is my favorite day so far," Kara said, straightening to guide the stroller through another group of costumed families.

Ryder kissed her head. "I think you say that every day."

"I do." She beamed. And it was true every time.

"Just make sure you say *that* next weekend."

"We'll see," she teased.

The six short days until the wedding felt more like six end-to-end eternities, and if brides were supposed to be nervous, then Kara was doing it wrong. The Garretts had stepped in to handle everything while she recovered in the early weeks after being released from the hospital. She'd had crutches for her ankle, and cream for her burns, but the Garretts had circled around her and Casey as if they were invalids, only asking what she wanted, then disappearing to get it done. She'd felt guilty at first for all the help, knowing she was capable of finding ways to do more. If it had been just her and Casey, she'd argued, then she would have had to do it all herself. The Garretts dismissed the argument. It didn't matter to them what might have been, only that she and Casey weren't alone now. They had family, and families got things done.

When she'd met Mrs. Garrett and Ryder's brothers' wives for lunch to make wedding plans, she'd seen it on their faces. They were happy to be a part of her life. They wanted to be there for this big day and all the others that followed. That was when it had finally sunk in. She had three sisters now, a set of parents living in town and cousins for Casey to grow up with.

"Here we are." Ryder smiled at the adorable display on Blake and Marissa's front porch.

A giant cauldron overflowed with candy on the top step. A happy ghost stood behind it with a sign instructing local ghouls and goblins to help themselves to two pieces each. A small print notation warned that the candy was monitored by a federal agent and taking more than two pieces constituted theft.

Kara snorted. "He must be a hit with the neighbors."

"Lucky for him everyone loves Marissa. If they didn't this place would be covered in toilet paper." Ryder rushed forward to swing the garden gate open at the side of the little bungalow.

There was no room for doubt as to where the party was: a trail of jack-o'-lanterns led them up the winding cobblestone walk all the way to the backyard.

West greeted them with open arms. He stood near the gate, watching a toddler in a pink princess dress waddle around a display of pumpkins and cornstalks. "Finally," he said. "Do you know how many times Mom has asked when you were coming?"

"Sorry, man," Ryder said, straight-faced. "Kara took forever to get dressed."

Kara shoved him, her cheeks heated with the

thinly veiled implication. "We're sorry we're late," she said. "We let Casey finish her nap before we tried to dress her in that marshmallow."

West stood back then, taking in the sight of them together. He hooked his thumbs in the thick over-all straps of his fishing waders. He shot a twisted grin at his brother. "What are you supposed to be? A two-by-four?"

"I'm a graham cracker," Ryder said, reaching out to flip the wide brim of West's bait-lined hat. "What are you? A fisherman? How original."

Tina made her way to West's side then, dressed as a fish, a baby sheriff in her arms. "Oh! You're here!" She hugged Ryder, then Kara. "I'm so glad to see you. Mrs. Garrett is about to explode from anticipation. Did you make it to the courthouse?"

Ryder held up a finger. "Hang on now. Your husband put on some waders, called it a costume, then made you come here as a fish?"

West slid an arm around Tina's waist. "She's a striped bass, and my best catch yet."

"Yet?" Tina asked, her perfect eyebrows arched high. "You're lucky I wasn't the one who got away."

West kissed her, successfully stanching her protest. Kara smiled as Tina took the bait.

Blake appeared then, a look of concentration on his face as he strode through the thick crowd of Garretts filling his little backyard. Marissa followed closely behind.

Kara tried not to laugh at his costume. If Ryder

thought West's was unoriginal, Blake's FBI badge and jacket over a T-shirt with jeans won the contest for not-even-a-costume. "Hey." She leaned forward for a hug when he arrived. "This is one heck of a party, Blake. Everything looks amazing. Food smells great. Music is perfect." She giggled as the *Ghostbusters* theme song began.

"Marissa and her sister," he said, a bag of suckers clenched in one hand. "They love this stuff. How's the candy situation looking out front?"

"Not as bad as that costume," Ryder said.

Blake shot him a droll look.

A loud squeal broke through the white noise, and West stepped to the side. "Here she comes."

Mr. and Mrs. Garrett, and Cole and Rita rushed across the lawn in single file toward them.

Mrs. Garrett was dressed as a life-size Raggedy Ann doll, complete with painted red cheeks and freckles. "Look at you," she cooed, dragging her happy gaze from Ryder, to Kara, to Casey. "How did it go?" she asked. "Did you have any trouble?"

"No." Ryder pulled Kara closer. "Casey's biological father had no problem signing off on her adoption. The lawyer drew up the papers, we signed and they'll be filed for us on the Monday after the wedding."

"More Garretts," she said in a hungry, theatrical voice, her fingers wiggling happily in front of her. "That's the best news I've heard all day."

"Agreed," Mr. Garrett said with a wide smile.

Blake raised his bag of suckers overhead. "To more Garretts."

"More Garretts," the little crowd echoed.

Tina shook her head. "There are so many things I could say about this family." Her psychologist's mind was clearly working as she smiled and laughed.

"No doubt," West agreed as Cole and Rita ran off. "Come on. Those two are about to bob for apples again." He rolled his eyes. "She lets him win, but he doesn't care."

Kara exchanged a pointed look with Tina and Mrs. Garrett, who burst into laughter.

"What?" Mr. Garrett freed Casey the Babbling Marshmallow from her stroller and lifted her into his strong grandpa arms.

"Nothing," the women said.

What the men didn't know wouldn't hurt them.

Ryder grabbed Kara's hands and pulled her into the mix of relatives and friends. He spun her against him as the "Monster Mash" began. He twined their fingers and kissed her lips beneath the crisscrossed strands of orange-and-purple twinkle lights. "Marry me," he whispered.

"Yeah." She stretched onto her toes and kissed him longer, deeper.

"I bet my mom would keep Casey for the night," he murmured against her lips.

Kara giggled.

Ryder pulled back an inch, holding her torso tight

to his. "I'll make the arrangements and swipe a bottle of wine from the buffet."

Her eyes and smile widened. "What do I do?"

Ryder gave her a sharp wink. "Don't take off that costume."

Kara covered her mouth with one hand and let the heat rise over her cheeks as she watched the big graham cracker steal wine and kiss his mom good-bye. He was back at her side in a flash, tugging her through the rear gate and along the quiet trail back to their neighborhood.

"I think this should be our new tradition," he said, stopping to kiss her again beneath an ancient oak tree.

Kara closed her eyes and let the kiss carry her away.

* * * * *

*Look for more books from
Julie Anne Lindsey later in 2019!*

*And don't miss the previous titles
in the Garrett Valor miniseries:*

Federal Agent Under Fire
The Sheriff's Secret
Shadow Point Deputy

Available now from Harlequin Intrigue!

#1839 HOSTAGE AT HAWK'S LANDING
Badge of Justice • by Rita Herron
Dexter Hawk's search for the truth about his father's death leads him to a homeless shelter where Melissa Gentry, the love of his life, works. Together, can they stop a dangerous conspiracy that has caused the disappearance of several transients in the area?

#1840 THE DARK WOODS
A Winchester, Tennessee Thriller • by Debra Webb
Sasha Lenoir has always wondered what happened on the night her parents died. Now she'll do anything to learn the truth, even if that means employing the help of US Marshal Branch Holloway—the father of the child she's kept secret for more than a dozen years.

#1841 TRUSTING THE SHERIFF
by Janice Kay Johnson
Detective Abby Baker can't remember anything from the past week. She just knows that someone tried to kill her. Placed under Sheriff Caleb Tanner's protection, can Abby recall what happened before her attacker strikes again?

#1842 STORM WARNING
by Michele Hauf
When a woman is killed, police chief Jason Cash wonders if the killer attacked the wrong person, since Yvette LaSalle, a mysterious foreigner with the same first name as the victim, seems to be hiding in the remote town. Can Jason protect Yvette from an unknown enemy?

#1843 UNDERCOVER PREGNANCY
by Alice Sharpe
Following a helicopter crash, Chelsea Pierce remembers nothing—not even the fact that Adam Parish, the man who saved her, is the father of her unborn child. With determined killers closing in, will Adam and Chelsea be able to save themselves...and their baby?

#1844 THE GIRL WHO COULDN'T FORGET
by Cassie Miles
Twelve years ago, Brooke Josephson and five other girls were kidnapped. Now Brooke and FBI special agent Justin Sloan must discover why Brooke's friend, another former captive, was murdered. Could the psychopath from her childhood be back and ready to finish what he started?

Get 4 FREE REWARDS!

We'll send you 2 FREE Books
plus 2 FREE Mystery Gifts.

Harlequin Intrigue® books feature heroes and heroines that confront and survive danger while finding themselves irresistibly drawn to one another.

FREE
Value Over
$20

He knew she was shaken, but he wasn't ready to let her out of his
sight. "Melissa, you could have been hurt tonight." Killed, but
he couldn't allow himself to voice that awful thought aloud. "I'll
see that you get home safely, so don't argue."

Melissa rubbed a hand over her eyes. She was obviously so
exhausted she simply nodded and slipped from his SUV. Just as
he thought, the beat-up minivan belonged to her.

She jammed her key in the ignition, the engine taking three
tries to sputter to life.

Anger that she sacrificed so much for others mingled with
worry that she might have died doing just that.

She deserved so much better. To have diamonds and pearls.
At least a car that didn't look as if it had been rolled twice.

He glanced back at the shelter before he pulled from the
parking lot. Melissa was no doubt worried about the men she'd
had to move tonight. But worry for her raged through him.

He knew good and damn well that many of the men who
ended up in shelters had simply fallen on hard times and needed a
hand. But others…the drug addicts, mentally ill and criminals…

He didn't like the fact that Melissa put herself in danger by
trying to help them. Tonight's incident proved the facility wasn't
secure.

The thought of losing her bothered him more than he wanted
to admit as he followed her through the streets of Austin. His gut
tightened when she veered into an area consisting of transitional
homes. A couple had been remodeled, but most looked as if they

were teardowns. The street was not in the best part of town, either, and was known for shady activities, including drug rings and gangs.

Her house was a tiny bungalow with a sagging little porch and paint-chipped shutters, and sat next to a rotting shanty, where two guys in hoodies hovered by the side porch, heads bent in hushed conversation as if they might be in the middle of a drug deal.

He gritted his teeth as he parked and walked up the graveled path to the front porch. She paused, her key in hand. A handcrafted wreath said Welcome Home, which for some reason twisted his gut even more.

Melissa had never had a real home, while he'd grown up on the ranch with family and brothers and open land.

She offered him a small smile. "Thanks for following me, Dex."

"I'll go in and check the house," he said, itching to make sure that at least her windows and doors were secure. From his vantage point now, it looked as if a stiff wind would blow the house down.

She shook her head. "That's not necessary, but I appreciate it." She ran a shaky hand through her hair. "I'm exhausted. I'm going to bed."

She opened the door and ducked inside without another word and without looking back. An image of her crawling into bed in that lonely old house taunted him.

He wanted to join her. Hold her. Make sure she was all right tonight.

But that would be risky for him.

Still, he couldn't shake the feeling that she was in danger as he walked back to his SUV.

Don't miss
Hostage at Hawk's Landing *by Rita Herron,*
available March 2019 wherever
Harlequin® Intrigue books and ebooks are sold.

www.Harlequin.com